OUTLAW RANGER

James Reasoner

Chapter 1

South Texas, 1900

Demons roamed the chapparal.

Not the sort that came from Hell, of course, although some might say this South Texas brush country bore a distinct resemblance to Hades, especially in the summer. It was hot as hell today, G.W. Braddock thought as he knelt with a Winchester in his hands and listened intently. He was a lean, sandy-haired man with a thick mustache of the same shade. A cloudless, brassy blue sky arched above him.

Somewhere out there in that brasada were Tull Coleman and his gang. Braddock had trailed them north from Corpus Christi where they had held up a bank and gunned down a young teller foolish enough to try to tackle one of Coleman's men. Then, as if for good measure, they had ridden down a young woman during their getaway, trampling and breaking her under their horses' hooves, leaving behind a grief-stricken husband and an 18-month-old daughter without a mama.

3

Braddock wished he could kill every one of the sons of bitches.

That wasn't his job, though. The star-in-a-circle Texas Ranger badge pinned to his faded blue shirt meant he just took them in. It was the responsibility of a judge and jury to mete out justice.

Of course, if he had to put bullets through a few of them in the process of making that arrest, it wasn't going to break his heart. There was also a little matter of self-defense. They wanted to kill him as much as he wanted to kill them—they had already shot his horse out from under him—and he had a right to try to stop them.

So come on, Tull, he thought. *Where the hell are you?*

A faint crackling sound drifted through the hot, still air. Something was moving in the brush to Braddock's right. It might be a javelina, he told himself...or it might be an owlhoot bent on shooting a Texas Ranger. Slowly, Braddock swiveled toward the sound and lifted the Winchester. His finger curled around the trigger.

One of the wild pigs that roamed this area burst out of the chapparal and lunged at Braddock, squealing. He didn't want to shoot and give away his position unless he had to, so he flung himself aside. The javelina rammed his left shoulder and he felt the animal's tusks tear through his shirt and scrape his hide. He was already a little off-balance, and the impact of the collision knocked him to the ground.

Several men charged out of the brush and whooped with excitement. One of them, a chunky hombre with a square head and black beard, kicked the Winchester out of Braddock's hands. Another tried to stomp his chest and cave in his ribs. Braddock caught hold of the man's boot just in time to save himself from that. He heaved on the outlaw's leg and toppled him over backward.

The fallen man got tangled up with the other two and that gave Braddock time to roll away from them and get up on his knees. He reached for the Colt on his hip, experiencing as he did so a split-second's worry that the gun might have fallen out of its holster while he was thrashing around on the ground.

Then his hand closed around the walnut grips and he felt the immense comfort of knowing that he was still armed. He pulled the Colt and shot the big, black-bearded man in the chest. The man rocked back a step as his eyes widened in surprise and then bugged out even more in pain. He felt of his chest where blood was welling out of the bullet hole as if to convince himself that he really was wounded.

Then he pitched forward on his face.

Before the bearded man hit the ground, Braddock had shifted the Colt and fired again, this time at a man with a fox-like face under a straw Stetson with a tightly curled brim that drooped down in front. Braddock's bullet struck him in his weak chin and angled up through his brain before blowing out the back of his skull. He dropped straight down, already dead.

That left the man who had tried to stomp Braddock. He scrambled onto hands and knees and then lunged to his feet and turned his back on the Ranger as he tried to flee. Clearly, all the fight had gone out of him now that his two companions were dead.

Braddock aimed this time instead of letting luck and instinct guide his shot. The third outlaw stumbled in his flight as Braddock's slug struck him in the small of his back and broke his spine. He tumbled to the ground and lay there screaming until he passed out about ten seconds later.

Braddock sat there breathing a little hard as he looked at the bodies scattered around him. He knew good fortune had been with him. Most men didn't survive three-to-one odds.

Unfortunately, there was a good chance three more outlaws still lurked out there in the thick brush...and one of them was Tull Coleman.

With the efficiency born of long practice, Braddock broke open the Colt and shook out the three empties, then thumbed fresh cartridges into the cylinder. He snapped it closed and pouched the iron. On hands and knees he crawled over to where his Winchester had landed. He picked it up and made sure the sandy ground hadn't fouled the barrel.

Fully armed again, Braddock resumed sitting and waiting. His pulse had slowed down a little now. A few minutes earlier, in the aftermath of the fight, it had been pounding fit to beat the band.

Every instinct in his body told him that Tull Coleman had been close enough to hear the three shots, followed briefly by the wounded man's screams. Coleman would be too curious to just let that go. He would have to come see what had happened.

The man with the bullet in his back groaned as he regained consciousness. When he fell, he had landed facing away from Braddock. Now he said, "Ranger...Ranger, are you there? I can't see you."

Braddock didn't reply. He didn't have anything to say to the outlaw right now.

"Ranger, I...I'm hurt mighty bad. I think my back's broke. I need help. You got to get me to a doctor."

That poor woman down in Corpus Christi had had

her back broken, too, along with plenty of other bones, when Coleman's gang stampeded over her. They could have swerved around her, but according to the witnesses Braddock had talked to, it had looked like Tull Coleman, who was in the lead, had ridden toward her on purpose. It was hard to believe that anybody could be that lowdown.

Braddock could believe it of Coleman, though. The outlaw had a reputation for violence and brutality, as did those who rode with him.

"Ranger? Ranger?...Oh, Lord, he shot me down and left me here to die. That star-packin' bastard." The wounded outlaw sobbed a couple of times, then raised his voice and called, "Tull! Tull, he ain't here no more! He shot me in the back and run off! I need help, Tull. I'm hurt bad."

The brasada was quiet. Even the little animals were silent, gone to ground because of the shots. The javelina that had knocked Braddock on his butt was long gone. The tusker hadn't even slowed down. Braddock was convinced that the three outlaws had spooked the animal and sent it charging through the brush in an attempt to flush him out.

That idea had backfired on them.

"Tull? I...I think Franklin and Tillotson are both dead. That damn Ranger bushwhacked us! We never had a chance."

Well, that was one way of explaining how come he'd been shot in the back, Braddock thought with a faint smile.

"Please..." The man's voice was weakening. He'd lost a considerable amount of blood and might well be on the verge of passing out. "Tull..."

Somebody or something moved in the brush.

The noises came closer. Braddock took advantage of them and retreated farther into the chapparal. The crackling covered any sounds his own movements caused. He stopped when there was a nice screen of mesquite branches between him and the wounded man.

A figure stepped out of the brush and bent over the fallen outlaw. He was short and stocky, a Mexican with his sombrero hanging behind his neck by its chin strap. Not Tull Coleman. Raul Gomez, Braddock decided. Gomez was on record as being one of Coleman's bunch.

"Jeff, you gone and got yourself killed," Gomez said.

"No, no, I'll be all right," the wounded man babbled. "I...I just need a sawbones."

"I don't think so. I seen men shot like that before. Even if you don't die, you won't never walk again, *amigo*. Better to go ahead and put you out of your misery right here and now."

Gomez shucked his Colt from leather and pointed it at the back of Jeff's head, clearly intending to blow his fellow outlaw's brains out. Braddock knew he ought to let Gomez go ahead and pull the trigger, but instead he stepped out of the brush, leveled his rifle, and said, "Hold it, Gomez."

The Mexican was turned half away from him. Gomez tried to twist around and bring up the revolver. Braddock squeezed the Winchester's trigger and sent a .44-40 round ripping through Gomez's lungs. The outlaw's Colt boomed as his finger contracted on the trigger, but the bullet tore harmlessly through the brush. The shot spun Gomez off his feet. He lay on the ground struggling to drag rasping, bubbling breaths into his body as he drowned in his own blood.

With a crash of brush, another man appeared to Braddock's left. He had a gun in each hand and fired both of them as fast as he could thumb the hammers back. He sprayed a lot of lead around, but rushing his shots like that, he failed to hit the Ranger with any of them. Braddock loosed another round from the Winchester, levered the rifle, fired again. Both shots punched into the outlaw's chest at close range. They lifted him off his feet and threw him backward.

With his ears ringing from all those shots, Braddock couldn't hear much of anything. So it wasn't a noise that warned him but rather instinct. He sensed someone coming at him from behind and tried to turn.

That movement was enough to cause the knife to merely rip a gash along his left collarbone instead of plunging into his back and skewering his heart. It still hurt like blazes and the pain drew a yell from Braddock's throat. He struck upward with the rifle butt and dug it under Tull Coleman's jaw. Coleman grunted but continued bulling against Braddock. The Ranger couldn't stay on his feet. Both men went down.

Coleman was wiry and fought like a wildcat. He slashed at Braddock with the Bowie knife in his hand. According to the reports the Rangers had, the heavy blade was Coleman's favorite weapon and he was good with it. Braddock had all he could do to block the knife with the Winchester's barrel, steel ringing against steel as he did so. The rifle's length made it awkward to handle in these close quarters, though, and Braddock knew it was only a matter of time before Coleman slipped past his guard and buried the Bowie in his guts.

Braddock let go of the Winchester with his right hand and shot that fist forward in a short but powerful blow that landed squarely on Coleman's nose. He felt cartilage crunch and flatten under the impact. Blood squirted hotly across his knuckles. Coleman's head rocked back from the force of the punch, and Braddock hit him again before he could recover.

While Coleman was half-stunned, Braddock cracked the rifle barrel against his wrist. That made Coleman drop the knife. Braddock lifted the Winchester and brought the butt down into Coleman's face, doing even more damage to the outlaw's bloody, battered features. Coleman went limp. He was either unconscious or dead, and at the moment Braddock didn't give a damn which.

Braddock planted the rifle butt against the ground and used it to help lever himself to his feet. With his chest heaving from all the exertion, he looked around at the six outlaws. Four of them were dead, he was pretty sure of that. Jeff was still alive. Braddock could hear his strained breathing. Coleman's chest rose and fell raggedly, so he was alive, too.

This had been a hell of a fight, Braddock thought. Six against one, and he was still alive and relatively unharmed. The gash on his back from Coleman's Bowie burned like fire, but Braddock didn't figure it was serious. If he was the sort to brag or be full of himself, he would say this was a legendary battle, the kind of fracas that folks would talk about for a long time to come.

But he didn't care about anything like that, only about bringing these killers and thieves to justice. That was his job, and he did it as well as he could.

However, he did allow himself one moment as he was reloading the Winchester to smile grimly to himself and say in a quiet voice, "How about that, Pa? That good enough for you?"

Chapter 2

Two days later, Braddock drove a wagon into San Antonio. He had commandeered it from a farm at the edge of the chapparal with a promise that it would be returned. Jeff Hawley, the outlaw he'd shot in the back, was still alive somehow and lay face down on a pallet of blankets in the wagon bed. Braddock had patched him up as best he could. Hawley was in and out of consciousness, incoherent much of the time when he was awake and cursing bitterly the rest of the time.

Tull Coleman was in the wagon bed, too, wearing shackles and leg irons. He didn't waste his breath cussing. Anyway, his jaw was still swollen from Braddock clouting him with the rifle butt, so it probably hurt to talk.

Braddock had left the bodies of the four dead outlaws with the marshal in the nearest town. The lawman had promised he would see to it that the men were buried, although the State of Texas would have to foot the bill, he'd warned. Couldn't ask the local undertaker to work for free. Braddock had agreed to that, although he didn't know if the request would be honored. All he knew was that he wanted the corpses off his hands. They would have stunk to high heaven if he'd had to take them all the way to San Antonio.

Braddock brought the team to a halt in front of the adobe building in Military Plaza that housed the headquarters of Company D. A couple of Rangers lounged near the entrance, puffing on quirlies and joshing with each other. They straightened and looked with interest into the back of the wagon.

"What you got there, Junior?" one of them asked.

Braddock's jaw tightened. He hated to be called Junior. Hadn't liked it when he was a kid, didn't like it even more now. But there was no denying that a lot of his fellow Rangers thought of him that way. It was unavoidable when he had the same name as his father.

The elder Braddock had been a sergeant in the Frontier Battalion under Major John B. Jones, the battalion's first commander. Sergeant George Washington Braddock Sr. had made a fine name for himself twenty-five years earlier, fighting outlaws and hostile Indians from San Antonio to El Paso. That was quite a legacy to live up to.

"Good Lord," the second Ranger exclaimed. "That's Tull Coleman, big as life."

"And twice as ugly," the first Ranger agreed. He let out a whistle of admiration. "Looks like you did a good job, Braddock. Lawmen have been lookin' for this varmint all over South Texas."

Braddock set the brake and climbed down from the wagon seat. His movements were stiff and awkward because his back still hurt where Coleman had cut him. He had started to wonder if the wound had festered.

"Captain Hughes inside?" he asked. When the two Rangers nodded, he went on, "Reckon you could see to locking up these boys? You'll have to take the wounded one over to Doc Sullivan's house and put a guard over him."

"Sure," one of the men said. "Say, Junior, have you heard the news?"

"News?" Braddock frowned. "What news?"

The other man nudged his companion and shook his head.

"You just go on in and report to the captain, Braddock. If he wants to tell you anything, he will."

Braddock didn't like the sound of that. Something was wrong, and he figured the quickest way to find out what it was would be to go inside and talk to the captain. He pointed to Coleman and told the other Rangers, "Keep a close eye on him. He's a tricky son of a bitch."

Braddock's boot heels rang on the polished wooden floor as a clerk showed him to Captain Hughes' office. Normally, the thick adobe walls meant it was cooler inside the headquarters building than out, but that didn't seem to be the case today. The air was hot and stifling, and Braddock had trouble getting his breath.

Captain John R. Hughes was built solid as a rock. His face was broad and sported a neat mustache. His brown hair was parted in the middle. When Braddock came in, Hughes stood up and reached across the desk to shake his hand.

"Private Braddock," Hughes said. "I got a telegram informing me that you were bringing in Tull Coleman and one member of his gang."

Hughes didn't ask him to sit, so Braddock remained standing. He nodded and said, "That's right, Captain. The other fella is Jeff Hawley. He's wounded, but he seems bound and determined not to die. Stubborn critter."

"What about the others who robbed that bank in Corpus?"

"They didn't want to come along peacefully," Braddock said, not offering any other explanation.

Hughes nodded slowly. "I see," he said. "That'll all be in your report?"

"Sure," Braddock replied with a shrug. He didn't care for writing reports, but he supposed it was just part of the job.

"That's good. Turn it in to me as soon as you're done." Hughes paused, drew in a deep breath, and went on with obvious reluctance, "I'm sorry to say that'll be your last official act as a Ranger, Private."

Braddock thought the air in here had gotten even hotter, and it made him so uncomfortable that for a moment he didn't comprehend what Hughes had just said. When the captain's meaning finally sunk in on his brain, he stared at Hughes and said, "You're kicking me out of the Rangers? What the hell for?"

Hughes' features tightened. Braddock knew the captain didn't like profanity, and his tone had been disrespectful, to boot. He felt too bad and was too angry to care. Hughes said, "This isn't my idea, Braddock. The Rangers are being disbanded."

That news was so shocking it made Braddock dizzy. He put a hand on the back of the chair in front of the desk to steady himself as he said, "That's loco, Captain. Why would Texas get rid of the Rangers?"

With his mouth twisting as if he had just bitten into a rotten apple, Hughes said, "It's not really the state's doing, either. It's all because of the lawyers."

Braddock shook his head and wished he hadn't,

because the motion just made him dizzier. "I don't understand."

"Some lawyer found something in the legislation that created the Rangers, back in 1874, that says only officers have the power to make legal arrests."

"I'm an officer," Braddock insisted. "An officer of the law."

"You're a private in the Texas Rangers. According to the letter of the law, you don't have the legal authority to do much of anything."

"I just brought in Tull Coleman and Jeff Hawley!"

Hughes sighed, shook his head, and said, "They'll probably have to be released. All the prisoners the Rangers have brought in who haven't already been tried and convicted are being let go. There are a dozen motions in the court to have those prior convictions vacated as well, but all that is still up in the air. For now all that really matters is that the Rangers are finished."

"No!" Braddock had to lean heavier on the chair to hold himself up. "No. My pa devoted his whole life to the Rangers. He raised me to be a Ranger. They can't be done away with because of some...some piss-ant lawyer!"

"I'm sorry, Braddock. It's out of my hands." Hughes paused. "Braddock? Are you all right? You look a little—Braddock!"

The captain's startled voice was the last thing Braddock heard. His head was spinning so bad it seemed like it was about to fly off his shoulders. He tried to brace himself on the chair but his fingers slid off. The floor jumped up and slammed him in the face.

That was the last thing Braddock knew for what seemed like a very long time.

* * *

"What the hell are you doin', cryin' over a damn dog?"

"He was my friend," George said as he patted down the dirt mounded on the grave he had dug himself. He tried not to sniffle. He knew his father hated crying, especially in men. Of course, at eight years old, he wasn't exactly a man, but Pa wouldn't care about that. He'd still fetch George a clout on the head if he got annoyed enough.

"He was a dumb animal. Couldn't be a friend to you nor nobody else. Jus' a dumb animal."

George didn't say anything. Arguing with his father really was pointless.

Pa kicked at the grave. "Get up and get on about your chores. The comp'ny's ridin' out tomorrow to hunt down some Mex bandidos. You'll have to keep the place goin' while I'm gone, same as usual. You know your ma's too sickly to do much." Under his breath he added, "And you ain't much better, boy."

George pretended not to hear. He got to his feet and turned to head for the barn. His father was right. There were chores to be done. He had to be dependable. Rangers were dependable, and he was going to grow up to be a Ranger. That was just the way of things.

But he couldn't stop himself from glancing back at the spot where he had laid his dog to rest. He started to mouth a farewell, and that was when he sensed his father's big hand coming at his head. George ducked the slap and broke into a stumbling run toward the barn.

"Get along with you!" the sergeant called after him. "Get along, you worthless little piss-ant! Good Lord, how'm I ever gonna make a Ranger out of a sorry specimen like you?"

Chapter 3

It was like being trapped in a mudhole, with the thick, slimy stuff trying to drag him under and clog his mouth and nose and drown him. Braddock fought desperately, clawing at the muck as it threatened to overwhelm him, and when he finally broke through the surface and gasped, he realized he wasn't drowning at all.

Instead he was lying in an airy room with big windows and cream-colored walls. The sheets underneath him were wet and uncomfortable. He lifted a trembling hand to his face and found that he was covered with beads of oily sweat.

Something moved to his right. From the corner of his eye, he saw a ghostly, white-clad figure drift into view. A middle-aged woman with a severe face leaned over him and said, "You're awake."

That seemed painfully obvious to Braddock. He opened his mouth and tried to speak, but his lips and tongue were too thick and clumsy to form words.

"I'll fetch Dr. Sullivan," the woman said as she

retreated from the bedside.

That told Braddock where he was, anyway, and the knowledge was a bit of a relief. He closed his eyes and concentrated on his breathing, which was a little erratic. As it settled into a steadier rhythm, he fought to stay awake. He didn't want to slip back into the hellish world where he had been.

The world of his own past.

A footstep made Braddock open his eyes again. A man with a close-cropped, salt-and-pepper beard had come into the room. Braddock recognized him. Dr. Alfred Sullivan said, "The nurse told me you were awake, Ranger Braddock."

Since he still couldn't talk, Braddock just shook his head.

Sullivan frowned in apparent confusion for a second, then understanding appeared on his face. "Now I know what you mean," he said. "That ridiculous business about the Rangers being disbanded." He reached for something on the bedside table. "Let's get you a drink."

He held a glass to Braddock's lips. Braddock had trouble swallowing, but he managed to get some of the water down his throat. He spilled some, too, but that didn't really matter since he was already soaking wet.

He was able to get a few words out after the drink.

23

"Wha...what happened...to me?"

"Blood poisoning from that knife wound in your back, I'd say," Sullivan replied. "You're lucky to be alive. You ran a very high fever for several days. But it's broken now. That's why you're sweating so much. I think you're going to be all right. You'll have to take it easy for a while because you're so weak, but with rest and good food you'll recover."

Braddock sighed and let his head sag back against the damp pillow. What was the point of getting better if he couldn't be a Ranger anymore?

From idle curiosity more than anything else, he asked, "How long...was I out?"

"It's been five days since you collapsed in Captain Hughes' office."

Five days, Braddock thought. Almost a week. Lord knew what had happened in that time.

Sullivan gave him another drink, then said, "I'll get Nurse Williams in here to clean you up and change the sheets on the bed, and then we need to see if you can take a little broth. You need to start getting your strength back as soon as possible."

Braddock didn't argue, but he didn't see why that mattered.

If he couldn't be a Ranger anymore, then nothing mattered.

* * *

Captain Hughes came to see Braddock the next day. In a hearty voice, he said, "I thought you'd up and died on me when you collapsed in my office that day, G.W."

Might have been better if he had, Braddock thought. He felt better and was stronger already as his iron constitution asserted itself, but he was in no mood for small talk. He said, "What happened to Coleman and Hawley?"

"They're still in custody. I arrested them myself before they could be released."

Braddock was glad to hear that.

Hughes paused, then went on, "I'm not sure how long we'll be able to hold them, though. A lawyer showed up and filed a motion saying they should be released since their original arrest was illegal."

Braddock was sitting up in bed, the wound on his back heavily padded with bandages. Anger stiffened him as he said, "Where in blazes are all these lawyers coming from? They're like cockroaches coming out of a hole!"

"You're not far wrong there," Hughes agreed. He pulled a ladderback chair closer to the bed and sat down. "The Rangers have made a lot of political enemies over the years, and some of them have plenty of money to hire lawyers to make things as difficult for us as possible. That's what's going on now. The governor's fighting back, though. I hear that instead of disbanding the Rangers, he's going to issue an order reorganizing the force. The Rangers will still exist, but our numbers will be cut drastically. Four companies of six men each, is the rumor I'm hearing."

"Twenty-four men to protect the whole state of Texas!"

Hughes shrugged. "Most people don't think the state needs that much protecting anymore. There hasn't been any Indian trouble in years, the border is pretty quiet right now, and most of what we do is chasing down outlaws. People say the county sheriffs and town marshals can handle that just as well. The Frontier Battalion has been too good at its job, G.W. Folks say we're just not needed anymore."

Braddock shook his head and scowled. He said, "They'll be singing a different song when it's their cattle that's been rustled or their loved ones who get gunned down by outlaws."

"You're probably right, but for now I'll be satisfied just to keep the Rangers in existence, no matter what form it's in. The legislature can write a new law to fix the problem in the old one, and then the Rangers can expand again."

One question in particular was nagging at Braddock, so he figured he might as well go ahead and ask it. "Captain...are you going to be able to keep me on as one of those twenty-four men?"

Hughes grimaced and then shook his head. "I wish I could, G.W. You've done a fine job. Your father would have been proud of you."

Braddock doubted that, doubted it very seriously.

"But the few spots we'll have will go to the Rangers who've been on the force the longest, in most cases," the captain went on. "If any of them don't want to keep their jobs, then we'll move on to the next man on the list. You've only been on Company D's rolls for a couple of years, though. I don't see how there would ever be a place for you...at least, not until the legislature passes that new law I mentioned and the force expands again. Then, maybe..."

"When will that be?"

"To be honest, there's no way of knowing. Like I said, the Rangers have political enemies, and they're more dangerous than outlaws. They'll try to block anything that might help us get back to normal."

"It's wrong," Braddock said. "It's all wrong."

"I agree with you, but there's nothing we can do except wait to see how the hand plays out."

Weariness washed over Braddock. He was too tired

to fight, too worn out to even talk about it anymore. He leaned back against the pillows propped behind him and said, "There's something over there on the dresser you need to take with you, Captain."

"What's that?" Hughes asked as he stood up. He looked down at the dresser, then back over at Braddock with a frown. "You're not talking about your badge, are you?"

"You said I wasn't a Ranger anymore. I don't need it, do I?"

Hughes picked up the star-in-a-circle badge and turned it over in his fingers. "You carved this yourself out of a Mexican peso, didn't you?"

"Yeah. That's what most of the fellas have done."

"Then it's yours. You need to keep it."

Hughes tossed the badge toward Braddock. Out of instinct, Braddock's right hand came up and caught it, plucking the badge deftly from the air. He wouldn't have thought he could react that quickly. He supposed his reflexes were coming back to him.

Hughes picked up his hat. "Don't worry about your medical expenses," he said. "Your injury happened in the line of duty, while you were still working for the State of Texas, so the state will pay for everything."

"Thanks," Braddock said. He couldn't keep a note of bitterness from creeping into his voice.

"I'll be in touch."

Braddock could tell that Hughes wanted to get out of there. He couldn't blame the captain for feeling that way. He just nodded without saying anything, and Hughes sighed and went out.

Braddock looked down at the badge lying on his palm. He stared at it for a long time and thought it was funny how a man's whole life could be shaped into a star and trapped inside a silver circle.

* * *

The next day, Braddock had a visit from a different lawman. The nurse brought a Bexar County deputy sheriff into the room. She looked uncomfortable and so did the deputy. The nurse got out as quickly as she could.

"How are you doin', Ranger?" the deputy asked.

"A little stronger every day," Braddock replied honestly. He felt like he would be almost back to normal in another week or so. He went on, "But I'm not a Ranger anymore. I reckon you probably know that."

"Yeah. That's, uh, sort of why I'm here." The deputy took a deep breath. "Mr. Braddock, I've got a warrant for your arrest. You'll be under guard here at the doctor's house until he says you're well enough to be moved."

Braddock felt like he'd been punched in the guts. Struggling to control himself, he said, "What are the charges on that warrant?"

"Murder, attempted murder, false arrest, and unlawful imprisonment."

"Who filed those charges?"

"I'm not sure I ought to answer that..."

Braddock said, "By God—", pushed the sheet back, and started to swing his legs out of bed.

The deputy held up a hand, palm out, to stop him. "It was a lawyer representin' Tull Coleman and Jeff Hawley. They say you ambushed them and killed four of their friends."

"They were outlaws! They robbed a bank in Corpus Christi and killed two people!"

"They're suspected of it, but no charges have been filed against them yet in Nueces County. That lawyer fella convinced the judge he had to let 'em go, since they'd been arrested illegally by, uh, you. And then he turned around and filed the charges against you. The sheriff says we've got to arrest you and let the whole thing run its course."

Braddock sat there stunned. It seemed as if everything in the world had gone wrong suddenly, that the way things were supposed to be had been turned on its head.

The deputy thumbed back his hat and went on, "I'll stay here with you until somebody relieves me. Hope you won't hold this against me."

Somehow, Braddock managed to shake his head and say, "You're just doing your job."

The deputy turned the chair around and straddled it. "Yeah, that's the way I'm tryin' to look at it, too, but I got to tell you, it's hard. I mean, hell, you're a Texas Ranger. That's what I wanted to be someday."

Thinking about what Captain Hughes had told him the day before, Braddock said, "It looks like we're both out of luck."

Chapter 4

The case against Braddock was heard by the grand jury a week later. That was pretty fast, due to a combination of circumstances. The grand jury happened to be in session, and Captain Hughes called in favors and used his influence to get Braddock's case moved up on the docket.

Braddock used a cane when he entered the courtroom, but he didn't really need it. The wound on his back had healed, the blood poisoning was gone, and most of his strength had returned to him. He wore a brown tweed suit he had bought for this hearing, all his other clothes being range garb. His shaggy hair was trimmed, and so was his mustache. His lawyer, a man named Dunaway whose fee was being paid by Captain Hughes personally, told Braddock that he looked properly respectful and respectable for court.

Grand jury proceedings were closed to the public, so the benches where spectators normally sat were empty. Braddock and Dunaway sat at one table in the front of the room while the district attorney sat at the other, along with Tull Coleman, Jeff Hawley, and their lawyer. Hawley was thin and pale and sat in a wheelchair, confirming Gomez's prediction that he would never walk again. Coleman had been cleaned up and looked hale and hearty, though. All the bruises had faded from his face. Seeing him there like that, free to walk the streets with an arrogant smirk on his face while all his victims were dead and buried, made Braddock's hands clench into fists.

If he'd had a six-gun right now, he would have been sorely tempted to blow both outlaws straight to hell, his own fate be damned. So it was probably a good thing they didn't allow people to be armed in the courtroom.

The judge came in and everybody stood up, Braddock leaning on the cane as he did so. Then the grand jury filed in and took their seats.

Braddock had testified before a grand jury once before, so he knew a little about how the proceedings worked. The district attorney presented the charges against him, then called witnesses, in this case Coleman and Hawley. Their testimony made it sound like they and their companions had been ambushed by Braddock with no warning and cut down ruthlessly by his shots.

The judge and the jury foreman interrupted now

and then to ask questions, usually pressing the witnesses for more details. It seemed obvious to Braddock that Coleman and Hawley were lying, and he hoped everybody else could see that, too.

Hawley testified with a quaver in his voice, though, and talked about what a rough time of it he'd had with legs that no longer worked, and Braddock thought he saw a little sympathy in the eyes of some of the jurors. That made him seethe inside, but he tried not to show it.

Coleman and Hawley were the only witnesses the district attorney had. Then it was Braddock's turn. When he was called to the stand, he started to use his cane, then changed his mind and left it lying on the table. He didn't need it, and damned it he was going to pretend that he did. He strode tall and straight to the witness chair.

After the bailiff had sworn him in, Dunaway asked him to tell his version of what had happened down there in the chapparal, about halfway between San Antonio and Corpus Christi.

"I got on the trail of the men who'd robbed the bank in Corpus and killed two people, then followed them into the brasada country," Braddock said. He nodded toward Coleman and Hawley. "Those two and four of their friends."

The outlaws' lawyer immediately objected. "There's no proof that my clients committed any crime," he insisted. "No charges have been filed against them."

"That's because they haven't been taken back to Nueces County where there'd be witnesses to what they did!" Braddock said.

The judge gaveled him to silence. "You're here to answer questions, Mr. Braddock, not to argue," he warned. "Confine yourself to that."

Anger made Braddock breathe a little harder, but he clamped his mouth shut and jerked his head in a nod.

"What happened when you pursued those men, Mr. Braddock?" Dunaway asked.

"They must have realized I was on their trail, because *they* bushwhacked *me*. They shot my horse out from under me, and I barely made it into the brush without getting ventilated. They came after me to try to kill me. I reckon they must've seen my badge and realized I was a Texas Ranger. They knew killing me was the only way they'd get me off their trail."

The other lawyer objected again on grounds of supposition. The judge sustained it, but Braddock thought he did so reluctantly.

With Dunaway prompting him, Braddock told the rest of the story, including the javelina. As he testified, he was aware of the badge resting in the breast pocket of his shirt. He seemed to feel it burning through his clothes, although that was impossible, of course. It was just silver. Nothing but inanimate metal. It didn't really glow with the hatred he felt, although sometimes in unguarded moments he imagined that it did.

When Braddock was finished, the jury foreman said, "Mr. Braddock, when all this occurred, you were a member of the Texas Rangers, is that correct?"

"Yes, sir. A sworn member of Company D of the Frontier Battalion."

"And you believed you were acting in a proper and lawful manner?"

"Yes, sir. Because I was."

The judge said, "We're not dealing with that issue here, Mr. Braddock."

"Sorry, Your Honor," Braddock muttered.

The jury foreman said, "You're aware that no one really knows what happened out there in the brush except you and these other two men? That it's your word against theirs?"

"The word of a Ranger against two murdering owlhoots, yes, sir, I know that."

That led to more outraged yelling by the lawyer for Coleman and Hawley. Braddock was sick of the whole business. He just wanted to get out of here. He wasn't sure where he would go or what he would do, but he was tired of everything being topsy-turvy.

Eventually the judge dismissed him. The evidence had been presented. There were no closing statements by the lawyers. The grand jury just headed off to figure out whether to indict Braddock on the charges and bind him over for a real trial.

Everybody else waited in the hall outside the courtroom.

Captain Hughes was there. He shook Braddock's hand and said, "How did it go in there?"

"I just told the truth, Captain."

Hughes nodded. "I don't doubt it. Anybody who knew your father would know you're an honest man, G.W."

Braddock's lips thinned. Captain Hughes had treated him decently. Had gone beyond that, really. It wouldn't serve any point to tell him what a dyed-in-the-wool bastard the senior Braddock had really been.

It seemed like the hearing had been over for only a few minutes when the bailiff called them back in. Clearly, it hadn't taken the jury members very long to figure out what they wanted to do.

The announcement was short and to the point, without any real drama to it. The foreman informed the judge that the jury was declining to present a true bill of indictment against George Washington Braddock, Jr. The judge nodded, said, "All charges against the defendant are dismissed," and whacked his gavel on the bench in front of him. "You're free to go, Mr. Braddock."

Dunaway grinned and shook Braddock's hand. Braddock didn't pay any attention to whatever the lawyer was saying. He looked past Dunaway at Coleman and Hawley, both of whom were stony-faced. Braddock saw the hate burning in their eyes, though, as they returned his stare.

He reckoned they saw the same thing in his gaze.

It would always be there.

* * *

A few days after the grand jury hearing, Captain Hughes came into the livery stable a couple of blocks from the Alamo while Braddock was getting his horse ready to ride. The scar on Braddock's back where Tull Coleman had cut him twinged a little as Braddock lifted the saddle onto the back of the dun he had purchased, but he ignored the discomfort.

"I heard you were leaving town, G.W.," Hughes said.

"Nothing to keep me here, is there? Now that I'm not a Ranger anymore, I mean."

"Do you have any work lined up?"

Braddock pulled the cinch tight and shook his head. "Not a bit."

"Where are you going?"

"Figured I'd drift west. See what turns up."

"That's not much of a plan," Hughes said with a worried frown.

"I never really had a plan except to carry a badge and enforce the law. Seems like that's over and done with now."

With a note of exasperation in his voice, Hughes said, "I told you, once the legislature passes a new law authorizing the expansion of the Rangers, you might be able to join up again."

"And when will that be, Captain?" Braddock wanted to know.

"Well, there's no telling," Hughes had to admit. "You know it takes a long time for things to go through channels, and like we talked about before, there'll be political enemies trying to stall anything that helps the Rangers."

"So maybe never," Braddock said dryly. "Blind hope doesn't sound like much of a plan, either, Captain."

"Blast it!" Hughes burst out. That was pretty strong language for him and showed that he was genuinely upset. "I know how these things go. I've seen it before. A man rides on one side of the law, and then something bad happens and he drifts over to the other side."

Braddock looked at the older man in surprise. "Captain, are you worried that I might turn owlhoot?"

"Things like that have been known to happen," Hughes said stiffly.

Braddock shook his head and said, "You don't have to worry about that. I was brought up my whole life to respect the law."

Even if I didn't respect all the men who enforced it.

"That's not going to change now. I'll never side with the owlhoots. Being a lawman is all I know."

"Well...maybe you can get a job as a deputy somewhere. Texas has settled down a lot, but there are still some rough places where a man like you could do some real good, G.W."

"I intend to do good," Braddock said. He meant every word of it, too. He pulled his Winchester part of the way out of the saddle boot to make sure it wasn't catching on anything, then slid it back in. He checked the pack of food and supplies tied on behind the saddle and nodded in satisfaction. His saddlebags were packed with things he would need, too, and a pair of full canteens hung from the saddle. As far as he could tell, he was ready to ride. "If there's nothing else, Captain...?"

"No, that's all." Hughes held out his hand. "Except to wish you good luck."

"Won't need it, but I appreciate that."

Braddock gripped the captain's hand and then swung up into the saddle. He lifted a hand in farewell as he rode out of the stable and turned the horse west.

San Antonio was such a big city it took him a while to reach the outskirts. Finally he put it behind him and started through the wooded hills that rose to the west and north. He paused on a rise and looked back but realized he wasn't leaving anything important behind him. He had everything he needed with him.

Including his badge, and when he thought about it he rested his hand briefly on his shirt pocket, smiling as he felt the hard shape under the cloth. The Rangers might not have any use for him anymore...

But that didn't mean he was through with the Rangers.

Chapter 5

Crockett County, Texas, two months later

More than thirty years earlier, the transcontinental railroad had been completed with the driving of the Golden Spike at Promontory Point, Utah, and in the decades since then the steel rails had spread out in a network that covered much of the territory west of the Mississippi.

The railroad hadn't come to Crockett County, though. The nearest rail line was the Southern Pacific, which ran through Comstock, sixty miles south of Ozona, which was not only the county seat but also the only settlement in Crockett County. But the Deaton Stagecoach Line ran from Ozona to Comstock, the line's Concord coaches making several trips back and forth each week. Comstock wasn't far from the Rio Grande and the terrain around it was mostly flat, but as the stage road ran north toward Ozona it entered more rugged territory marked by limestone ridges covered with scrub brush, cactus, and mesquite trees.

Today a southbound coach had just gone through a

gap in one of those ridges. The gray-bearded jehu, Ben Finley, kept the team of six sturdy horses at a steady, ground-eating trot. Finley knew better than to run the horses. At best, George Deaton, the line's owner, would dock a driver's pay if he found out the man had been running the teams. At worst the driver would find himself quickly out of a job. That was understandable since those horses were the life's blood of the company.

Still, there were always special circumstances. This was one of them, Ben Finley realized as he heard gunshots over the pounding of the horses' hooves and looked back to see several riders galloping after the stagecoach. He knew they must have been hidden in the clump of boulders just south of the gap.

Finley shouted at the horses and slashed the long reins across the rumps of the wheelers. The team lunged ahead, jolting the coach and making it rock violently on the broad leather thoroughbraces that supported it. Shouts of alarm came from inside the coach.

Finley had five passengers on this run: two whiskey drummers with orders to fill from Ozona's numerous saloons; a young woman of dubious reputation; a young cowboy who had spent the trip so far ogling the soiled dove; and Rudolph March, a Crockett County rancher on his way to Comstock to catch the train to El Paso where he intended to conduct some business. Finley had toted enough such passengers in his years driving a stagecoach that he felt like he knew all these people, whether he had ever seen them before or not.

"Hold on, folks!" he yelled back at them. "It's liable to get a mite rough!"

That was putting it mildly. The stagecoach road was in pretty good shape because the Deaton family kept it maintained, but ruts were inevitable and a coach traveling this fast was going to feel each and every one of them. Finley bounced on the seat as the vehicle careened along.

He had an old Colt Navy .36 in a crossdraw holster on his left side, and he wished he could pull the gun and turn around to blaze away at the pursuers. That might discourage them. He wished George Deaton paid somebody to ride shotgun on his coaches, too, but that seemed like an unnecessary expense to the boss. Nobody had tried to hold up one of these coaches in years.

But it was happening today, and Finley felt his heart thud in fear as he glanced back and saw the horsebackers gaining on him. They had their hats pulled low and bandannas over their faces, so that seemed to answer any questions about whether or not they were bandits out to hold up the stage.

More shots boomed, closer this time, and Finley twisted around to see the young cowboy hanging out the coach's window and firing back at the outlaws. The cowboy's body jerked suddenly as the gun slipped from his fingers. He slumped forward, his arms hanging down and his head and shoulders still outside the window while the rest of him remained in the coach. Finley could tell by the way youngster's arms swayed limply that he'd been hit and probably was dead.

The jehu bit back a curse and lashed the horses again. The same fate that cowpoke had suffered might be waiting for all of them if they didn't get away.

The road curved around more boulders up ahead, so Finley didn't see the men waiting there for the stagecoach until it was too late. They spurred their horses out into the open, firing as they came, and Finley was driven back against the coach by the slugs pounding into his body. The reins slipped from his fingers as pain flooded through him. Knowing that he was only moments away from death, he clawed at the Colt. He wanted to take at least one of the bastards with him when he crossed the divide.

Instead he passed out and slid down onto the floorboards to die there. The team kept running until one of the men on horseback caught up to the leaders and leaned over from his saddle to grab the harness and haul back on it. The horses slowed and gradually came to a stop.

The other riders had caught up by now. They all surrounded the coach. A shot blasted from inside the vehicle as Rudolph March put up a fight. After carving out a living on the Texas frontier for so many years, it was all the old rancher knew how to do.

He paid for that stubborn resolve with his life as the outlaws opened fire and hammered the coach with their lead. The thin walls didn't stop very many of the slugs. March fell back out of the window as blood spouted from the holes in his chest. The two drummers screamed even louder than the whore as they tried to hug the floor and escape the storm of bullets.

After a few seconds, one of the bandits waved an arm and shouted an order over the gun-thunder. "Hold your fire! Stop shooting, damn it!"

The guns fell silent as their echoes rolled away over the hills. The leader motioned to one of the other men and said, "Open that door, Wiley."

Cautiously, the outlaw approached the stagecoach, leaned over from his saddle, and twisted the handle on the door. As he flung it open, a body that was slumped against it inside toppled out, sliding all the way to the ground. The whiskey drummer landed on his back with his arms outflung, his sightless eyes staring at the sky. The front of his vest and shirt were sodden with blood.

"Don't shoot! Oh, God, please don't shoot!"

The plea came from the other drummer. The leader of the outlaws pointed his gun at the open door and ordered, "Come on out of there."

The surviving drummer crawled out of the coach and clung to the door for support as his rubbery legs threatened to fold up underneath him. He was pale and sweating but didn't appear to be wounded.

"Anybody else in there?" the boss outlaw demanded.

"Only a girl...a...a whore...and she's dead."

The boss inclined his head toward the coach and said, "Make sure he's telling the truth."

A couple of the bandits dismounted, grabbed the quaking drummer, and flung him to the ground several yards away from the coach. Then as one of them leaned into the vehicle through the door, a pop sounded. The man jerked back and yelled a curse. He clapped a hand to his left ear. Blood ran between the fingers.

"Bitch's got a derringer! She damn near shot my ear off!"

The gun must have been a single-shot weapon. The wounded outlaw reached into the coach and dragged out the screaming, struggling soiled dove. He dumped her on the ground next to the dead drummer.

"So she's dead, is she?" the leader said to the surviving drummer. "She looks mighty alive to me."

He raised his gun as the drummer frantically tried to scoot backward on his butt. He yelled, "No! No!" but it didn't do any good. The leader's gun roared and the drummer's head snapped back as a red-rimmed hole appeared in his forehead. He collapsed and didn't move again.

The boss outlaw holstered his gun and then pulled down the bandanna mask over the lower half of his face, revealing his lean, beard-stubbled features. He smiled as he said, "We'll take the girl with us. A little extra loot."

The man whose ear had been mangled said, "I oughta get first turn with her. I'm the one she shot."

"I don't know," the boss said with a grin. "You might be too ugly now. Might offend her delicate sensibilities. But I'll think about it." He turned to the others. "Get the box down and bust it open. We'll see what we find. I know March is carrying some money. He was talking in the saloon in Ozona about how he planned to buy some prime bulls from a rancher in

Mexico. However much we get, it's a good start."

He dismounted and went over to the young woman. She cowered away from him, but he bent down, grasped her arm, and jerked her to her feet. His fingers dug cruelly into her flesh through her sleeve and made her wince.

"Don't give us any more trouble and you'll come through this a whole lot better," he warned her. "I'm not saying you'll enjoy it, but it'll be a lot less painful."

"I...I'll do whatever you say, mister," she stammered. "Just don't kill me."

"Why, shoot, you'll be fine," he said as he smiled down at her. "I give you my word on that. And everybody knows you can take ol' Tull Coleman at his word."

Chapter 6

Braddock rode into Ozona while the town was in a hot, sleepy, midday haze. Folks had retreated into the mostly adobe buildings in search of relative coolness. Nothing moved on the street except the tails of a few horses tied at hitch rails as they tried to swat away flies. Braddock angled his dun toward one of those rails in front of the Splendid Saloon.

He hoped the place lived up to its name, but he wasn't counting on it.

He was leaner, his features more drawn since the day he rode away from San Antonio nine weeks earlier. In that time he had drifted around considerably, visiting Eagle Pass and Del Rio, then swinging north to San Angelo and Abilene, back around to Brownwood, Kerrville, and Bandera, making a wide circle through southwestern Texas. During that time he had kept his ears open, buying dozens of beers, asking questions, listening to what anybody had to say.

He hoped that effort was about to pay off.

He went into the saloon and thumbed back his hat as he stood at the bar that ran down the right side of the room. There were a dozen men in the place, half of them engaged in a desultory poker game at a big round table. Two of the others sat at a table nursing drinks, while the other four leaned on the bar and argued without much enthusiasm about the results of a recent horse race.

A craggy-faced bartender drifted along the hardwood until he was across from Braddock. "Get you something, mister?" he asked.

"Beer's fine," Braddock said.

The bartender filled a mug and set it in front of Braddock, who slid a silver dollar across the mahogany.

"Beer's only four bits," the bartender said.

"I'm paying for the company," Braddock said.

The bartender grunted. "Trust me, it ain't worth that much. You ridin' the grub line?"

"What makes you think that?"

"You look like you know your way around cows," the man replied with a shrug. "And you're not from around here. I'd remember you if you were."

"I can set a horse, but I've never worked cows in my life," Braddock answered honestly. The only job he'd ever had was as a lawman.

The bartender swiped a rag over the hardwood and said, "Well, it's none of my business."

Sensing the man was about to turn away, Braddock said, "I heard you had some trouble around here not long ago."

"Here in Ozona, you mean? I don't recollect any."

"I'm talking about the stage holdup between here and Comstock. It's got folks in this part of the country stirred up."

"Oh." The bartender nodded. "Well, that's true enough, I suppose. That was a bad thing. A mighty bad thing."

"Outlaws killed the driver and all the passengers on the stage, is that right? Something like six people in all?"

"Yeah." The bartender blew out his breath in a disgusted sigh. "Took a while for the sheriff's posse to find the body of the gal they carried off, and when they did I reckon they wished they hadn't. Those bastards tore her up real bad, I heard. Finding her didn't do a thing for her, just gave some of those possemen nightmares."

"They were able to give her a decent burial," Braddock pointed out.

"Yeah, there's that, I suppose. But I wouldn't have wanted to see what they did to her."

"The sheriff couldn't trail the men who were responsible for what happened?"

"He tried, but to tell you the truth, after seein' the way they slaughtered those folks, I'm not sure he was too keen on catchin' up to 'em, if you know what I mean."

Braddock nodded and sipped the beer, which was surprisingly cool.

The bartender grinned. "Good, ain't it? We've got an ice house here in town. I keep my kegs sittin' on a block of ice all the time. Coldest beer between San Antonio and El Paso."

"Splendid," Braddock said dryly. That just made the bartender's grin get bigger. It disappeared, though, when Braddock went on, "Have you heard any rumors about who might have pulled that stagecoach robbery?"

"Say, you're mighty interested in that, ain't you?" the bartender asked. "What business is it of yours?"

Braddock reached into his shirt pocket and then laid his hand on the bar. When he turned it up a little, he revealed his badge lying on the hardwood.

The bartender's eyes widened. "Ranger, huh?"

"G.W. Braddock." There was a note of pride in Braddock's voice as he introduced himself.

"I heard the Rangers got put out of business."

"In this world, you hear a lot of things that aren't necessarily true," Braddock said. His tone was flat and hard now. He covered up the badge again and then slipped it back into his pocket. "I know Tull Coleman has put together a new gang and is operating around here. If you have any idea where I might be able to find him, you'd better tell me if you know what's good for you."

"Why in the hell would I know where Tull Coleman is?" the bartender asked. He tried to put some bluster and bravado in his voice, but the attempt wasn't very successful. His words were loud enough, though, to draw some attention from the men down the bar.

"I imagine folks from all over this part of the country drink in this saloon. If you keep your ears open, there's no telling what you might hear."

With a surly frown, the bartender said, "A man who keeps his ears open is smart to keep his mouth closed."

Braddock sighed. He had just about run out of patience. He said, "If you've heard anything—"

The bartender didn't let him finish. "Sorry, Ranger. I don't know a damned thing."

If that was the way he wanted to be...

Braddock's left hand shot across the bar. He grabbed the front of the bartender's shirt and twisted, tightening his grip. Then he jerked the man halfway onto the bar, upsetting the mug of beer that sat there. The bartender wasn't a small man, but Braddock had taken him by surprise.

The bartender shouted in alarm. Braddock pulled his gun with his other hand and slammed it across the bartender's face, stunning him. Several of the men in the saloon yelled angrily. Braddock maintained his hold on the bartender as he turned and swung his Colt to cover the other patrons.

The two men who'd been drinking at a table were halfway to their feet. The ones playing poker just stared in surprise and confusion. The four men at the bar looked like they wanted to rush Braddock, but staring down the barrel of a Colt put a damper on their enthusiasm in a hurry.

"Just stay where you are, gents," Braddock warned. "This is law business."

"Better do what he says," the bartender mumbled. His voice was thick because his lips were swelling where Braddock had hit him. "He's a Ranger."

That brought murmurs of surprise from several of the men. Braddock supposed they had heard the rumors about the Rangers being disbanded, too.

One of the men at the bar said, "I didn't think a Ranger would pistol-whip an innocent man for no good reason."

Braddock let go of the bartender, who slid off the hardwood to the floor behind it. He didn't lower the revolver as he said, "When I'm on the trail of murderers, there are no innocent men. I'm looking for the animals who butchered everybody on the Comstock stage, and anyone who gets in my way better look out for himself. Best way to do that is to help me find the men I'm after."

The bartender used his rag to wipe blood from his mouth. He said, "Listen, Ranger, a man could get hisself killed telling tales about Tull Coleman."

Mutters of agreement came from some of the other men.

"So he and his bunch *have* been seen around here," Braddock said.

"Nobody's gonna tell you a damned thing," the bartender snapped. "We've all got wives, families."

"What about the men on that stagecoach? Did they have families? What about that woman? She may have been a whore, but does that mean she deserved what they did to her?"

Surly silence met Braddock's angry questions, but a few of the men at least lowered their eyes as if they were a little ashamed of their reluctance to help him.

That was all right. Braddock hadn't really expected any answers. That wasn't why he'd asked the questions.

Putting a tone of disgust in his voice, he said, "I can see I'm not going to get any help here. I'll just have to find Coleman on my own. But I will. You can damned well count on that."

He backed toward the door and through the batwings before holstering his gun. He jerked the dun's reins loose from the hitch rail and stepped up into the saddle, then turned the horse and rode at a fast lope out of town.

Braddock didn't stop until he was at the top of a small hill just north of Ozona. From here he could see the entire settlement and the area around it. He dismounted and waited, and less than half an hour later his patience was rewarded by a thin column of dust curling upward west of town. One rider, by the looks of it, and Braddock could tell that the man was in a hurry.

That was exactly what Braddock expected.

News of the stagecoach robbery had spread quickly, probably because the actions of the bandits had been so bloody and brutal. As soon as Braddock had heard that one of the murdered passengers was a well-to-do cattleman who'd been on his way to El Paso with a considerable amount of cash to conduct business, his instincts had told him that Coleman knew Rudolph

March would be on that stagecoach.

That meant Coleman had a confederate in Ozona tipping him off. Such an arrangement wasn't uncommon at all. Outlaws ruled by fear, and they also had friends and relatives scattered across the country who helped them out. That had been proven time and time again, going all the way back to the days of Jesse James and Sam Bass.

Confident that was the situation here, too, Braddock had gone into Ozona, thrown his weight around, announced that he was a Ranger, and declared his intention of finding Tull Coleman, all for the purpose of spooking whoever was working with Coleman. Braddock had no doubt that the rider he saw raising the dust in the distance was that man.

He reached into his pocket and took out the Ranger badge, pinning it to the front of his shirt. He didn't want anybody mistaking who he was or what he was after.

He was the law, and justice was his goal.

He swung up onto the dun and set out after his quarry.

Chapter 7

The road ranch belonged to a man called Augustus Vanderslagen, who had given it a name too long and foreign for most folks to remember. So they just called it Dutchman's Folly. Nobody thought the place would last long, out in the middle of nowhere between Ozona and Fort Stockton.

But its sheer isolation proved to be advantageous for those who wanted a place to stop over while they were riding lonely trails and didn't want to draw attention to themselves but desired a drink of decent whiskey, a hot meal, an actual bed, and maybe some female companionship, depending on whether Vanderslagen had any whores working for him at the moment.

Jeff Hawley had been here for several weeks. He spent his days brooding over a chess board set up on a table in one of the back corners of the low-ceilinged room. He had learned to play as a youngster, before the lure of easy money had seduced him into a life of outlawry.

Yeah, easy money, he sometimes thought bitterly. All it had cost him was half of himself. The half that was dead from just above his waist all the way down to his toes, which might as well not have even been there for all the feeling he had in them.

The chess set was missing a black knight and a white bishop. Lord knows what had happened to them. Hawley had talked Rosaria, the young, half-Mexican, half-Comanche whore, into finding a couple of distinctive-looking rocks he used in place of the missing pieces. He leaned forward in his wheelchair and hunched over the board, setting up problems and then working them out, all the while sipping from a glass of tequila that Rosaria refilled now and then. The fiery liquor kept the pain at bay and allowed Hawley to concentrate. At least he *thought* he was concentrating. He wasn't sure but what he was really in a drunken stupor and just didn't know it.

Today the pain in his back was worse than usual, so he'd been drinking more than he normally did. Rosaria watched him from behind the rough bar, which was nothing more than planks laid across whiskey barrels. She was leaning forward so that the low neckline of her blouse drooped enough to reveal practically all of her smooth brown breasts.

Hawley knew she wasn't really trying to be

provocative. He might have appreciated the view if he could do anything about it, but just like walking, that had ended the day G.W. Braddock put a bullet through his spine. Rosaria had tried every trick she knew to make him a man again—and she knew a lot—but nothing worked. Hawley had given up on that.

A man missing so much from his life had to have *something* to hang on to. With Hawley it was the determination that one day he would kill that bastard Braddock.

After staring at the chess board for a while, he reached out and moved the pink rock that took the place of the white bishop. He was trying to figure out black's best move in response when he heard the swift rataplan of hoofbeats approaching the low, sprawling adobe building.

Behind the bar, Rosaria heard the horse, too. She straightened and looked worried. She and Hawley were the only ones in the barroom. Vanderslagen was in a back room, sleeping off the previous night's sodden binge.

Hawley didn't blame Rosaria for being concerned. A fast horse usually meant trouble. An eighteen-year-old whore and a cripple might be tempting targets for that trouble. It sounded like only one rider was galloping toward Dutchman's Folly, so there was that to be thankful for, at least.

Hawley reached under the blanket that covered his useless legs and brought out a .38 caliber top-break Smith & Wesson revolver with ivory grips. All five chambers in the revolver's cylinder were loaded. Unlike some men, Hawley never worried about carrying the hammer on a live round. If he accidently shot himself, hell, he'd never feel it, would he? And if he bled to death he wouldn't be losing much...other than the chance to have his revenge on the man who had crippled him, and it seemed pretty unlikely that would ever come about.

He set the gun on the table next to the chess board. As bleak as his thoughts were, his situation hadn't completely eroded his natural defiance. If somebody wanted a fight, by God, Jeff Hawley would give him one.

He jerked his head at Rosaria and told her, "Get on in the back."

"I can get the Dutchman's shotgun—"

"No. Just go on back there, and don't come out no matter what you hear."

"You're sure?"

"Go, damn it," Hawley told her as the running horse came to a stop outside.

Rosaria scurried out from behind the bar, went past

him, and disappeared through the beaded curtain over the rear hallway.

Hawley glanced down at the chess board one last time, muttered, "Oh, hell, of course," and moved a black rook. He put a finger on the white queen and tipped it over. Checkmate.

A man stepped into the open doorway, starkly silhouetted by the late afternoon sunlight behind him.

Hawley relaxed slightly. Anybody out to kill him who was any good wouldn't have made himself such an easy target.

"Hawley? You in there? Good Lord, it's dark as a bear cave in here. Smells about as bad, too."

Leaning back in his wheelchair, Hawley said, "Damn it, Jennings, I nearly shot you. Don't you know better than to come rushing up to a place like that?"

The newcomer walked on into the room. Hawley could see him better now and recognized the stocky figure, the beefy, flushed face. Edgar Jennings owned one of the stores in town. He drank too much, ate too much, and liked money too much. He was also one of Tull's distant relatives by marriage, all of which explained his willingness to help out the gang by providing information. He was the one who had told Hawley about Rudolph March's business trip to El Paso.

"What are you doin' out here?" Hawley went on. "If you've got some other tip you want me to pass on, it's too soon. Tull said he wanted to lay low for a few weeks after hittin' that stagecoach."

Jennings shook his head and said, "No, it's nothing like that. A man rode into town today looking for Tull. He started asking questions in the saloon, and he roughed up Brodie and waved a gun around."

"Who the hell would do something like that?"

"He said he was a Texas Ranger."

"That's—" Hawley began. He'd been about to say that was crazy before he stopped. He resumed, "There aren't any Rangers anymore. The state did away with 'em." Again he paused. "Well, all but a few..."

Hawley's frown deepened. The Rangers had been chopped down to practically nothing, that was true enough...but from what he'd heard, a few of them remained on the job. He supposed it was possible one of them was trying to pick up Tull's trail.

"What did this fella look like? Did you see him?"

"Yeah, I was playing poker in the Splendid when he came in. He was tall, sort of long and ropy, but tough looking. Had light brown hair and a mustache."

That could have described a lot of men in Texas, but it sounded like one in particular to Hawley, one he had very good reason to know—and hate.

"Now I'm sure this is loco," he said. "That's G.W. Braddock. He's not a Ranger anymore. I am pure-dee certain of that, Edgar."

Jennings shrugged and said, "I'm just telling you what happened." He frowned. "Braddock...ain't he the one who—"

"Yeah," Hawley cut in. He gripped his chair's wheels and rolled it back from the table. "If he's going around telling people he's a Ranger, he's lying. That damn grand jury wouldn't indict him, but he lost his badge, no doubt about that."

"Brodie says he saw the badge."

Hawley scrubbed a hand over his face. Thoughts wheeled crazily through his brain. This didn't make any sense. Had Braddock gotten back into the Rangers somehow? Or was he just pretending to be a lawman?

And the most important question of all...

Where the hell was he now?

"What happened after that dust-up in the saloon?" Hawley snapped. "Where did he go?"

"Hell, I don't know. He rode out of Ozona heading north."

Hawley thought about the terrain around the settlement, and as he did, his worry grew.

"There's a hill up there where Braddock could watch the town," he said. "If that's what he did, there's a good chance he saw you ride out, Edgar."

Jennings' eyes got big with alarm. "You think that's what he did? Son of a bitch! He could have followed me. He could have...could..."

As his voice trailed off, Jennings started shaking his head and backing away.

"Yeah," Hawley said coldly, "he could have."

He picked up the Smith & Wesson, and as rage flooded through him he fired the revolver five times, emptying its cylinder. Jennings jerked every time one of the .38 caliber slugs punched into his chest. He took a step back, then another, then swayed from side to side as crimson threads of blood trickled from both corners of his mouth. He whimpered once like an animal in pain before he toppled over, upsetting an empty table and a couple of chairs. His face scraped along the rough, splintery planks of the floor, leaving a bloody welt on his cheek, but he never felt it.

Because of the low ceiling, the shots sounded even louder than usual. Hawley's ears rang. He looked down at the empty gun in his hand and realized how his anger had made him stupid. He couldn't hear very well, and the revolver was just a useless hunk of metal when it didn't have any bullets in it. He broke it open from the top, dumped the empty brass on the table, and fumbled in the pocket of his vest for fresh rounds.

"Bad idea, Jeff," a voice said, sounding muffled because Hawley's ears were still affected by the shots but clear enough to understand. Two figures moved around the table into Hawley's line of sight. One of them was Rosaria.

The other was G.W. Braddock, and he had his left arm looped around the whore's neck, holding her tightly against him. His other hand held a Colt pointed at Hawley.

"You're not..." Hawley began. "You can't be..."

Braddock pulled Rosaria to the side enough to reveal the star-in-a-circle badge pinned to his shirt.

"That's right," he said. "A Texas Ranger."

Chapter 8

Once Braddock was reasonably sure the man he had followed from Ozona was heading toward the lonely adobe building, he swung off the trail and circled wide to come up on the place from the rear.

It looked like the center part of the building had been constructed first, with a few extra rooms added on around it in a haphazard fashion. There was a pole corral in back, as well as a long, crude shed where any horses in the corral could get out of the brutal sun. Set at an angle away from the rear corner of the building was a privy.

The corral held only two horses at the moment, and neither of them paid any attention to Braddock as he rode up. There was a back door, but no windows on this side of the building. Braddock didn't even see any loopholes in the wall through which rifles could be fired to defend the place.

That wasn't important anymore, he reminded himself. Indians hadn't caused any trouble in this part of Texas for more than a decade. The only area where renegades were still a problem was out in the Big Bend, where Apaches sometimes raided across the border from their strongholds in the mountains of Mexico.

Like Captain Hughes had said, the Frontier Battalion had done its job too well.

Right now, however, Braddock was glad that whoever owned this place hadn't made it easy to defend. He was able to sneak up on it without being seen.

The back door had a simple string latch. Braddock drew his Colt and used his other hand to unfasten the door. It swung open on leather hinges that had dried out and hardened like iron in this hot, arid climate.

The hallway inside the door was dim and shadowy. Braddock saw some light at the far end where a beaded curtain separated the hall and the main room. A smell of stale beer and whiskey hung in the air. This was a road ranch, Braddock realized, where travelers could stop for a drink or a meal.

It wasn't on a main route, though, which made Braddock think that most of the men who stopped were probably on the dodge from the law. That wouldn't be as lucrative a trade as it once was—again, the Frontier Battalion of the Rangers had been successful at cleaning up a lot of the bandit gangs—

but there would always be lawbreakers looking for somewhere to hide out and rest up.

Braddock eased the door closed behind him and started toward the rectangle of light at the far end of the hall. He paused as a raucous snore came from an open door on his right. A grim smile tugged at the corners of his mouth. If whoever was in there was lucky, he would continue sleeping through whatever was about to happen.

A whisper of sound behind him was the only warning he had. He whipped around in a crouch as a figure lunged toward him. There was just enough light in the corridor for him to see a knife coming at him. Braddock ducked and twisted, and the blade went harmlessly over his left shoulder. Thrown off balance by the miss, the knife-wielder stumbled against him.

Braddock started to bring his gun down on the attacker's head, but he stopped the motion as he realized the body pressed to his was soft and curved, not to mention considerably shorter than him. He wasn't going to pistol-whip a woman.

But he wasn't going to let her stab him, either. As she drew the knife back for another try, he grabbed her wrist and twisted. At the same time he rammed his Colt back in its holster and clamped that hand over the woman's mouth so she couldn't cry out. He was pretty rough about it, he supposed, but that was better than bashing her head in.

The knife slipped from her fingers and thudded to the floor. Braddock grimaced at the sound, but he hoped it went unheard because by now men were talking out in the main room. The woman continued to struggle, but she stopped when Braddock turned her around and got his left arm around her neck. His forearm pressed against her throat like an iron bar. He could crush her windpipe or even break her neck without much effort, and she must have realized that.

He drew his gun again, put his lips against her ear, and whispered, "Just keep quiet and you won't get hurt."

He felt her try to nod. She was agreeing with him. He wasn't going to put any faith in that agreement, though, so he didn't ease up on his hold.

The only thing he had any real faith in was the badge pinned to his shirt.

* * *

George's father slapped the little paperbound book on the table and declared, "That's the only Bible you'll ever need right there, son. The Ranger's Bible. The Book of Knaves."

"The New Testament?" George asked.

The elder Braddock roared with laughter. "Not hardly! That's a list of all the outlaws on our books. We cross 'em off as we bring 'em in...or kill 'em."

"You shouldn't call it a Bible," George said with a frown. "Ma would say that's disrespectful to the Lord's Word."

"Your ma's been gone three years," his pa replied with a snarl. "I never let her tell me what to say or do while she was alive, neither. I sure as hell ain't gonna let some damn button do that."

He started to stand up, obviously expecting George to duck. George didn't, though. Since he'd started to get some growth on him, he'd stopped cringing as much. He figured his pa could still whip him six ways from Sunday if he wanted to, but George would deal out some punishment of his own in the process.

George's father pointed a finger at him and said, "One of these days, boy. One of these days you're gonna sass me one too many times, and then you'll be sorry."

"I didn't sass you, Pa. I just don't like the idea of calling a list of outlaws a Bible."

"You want truth?" The elder Braddock rested a blunt fingertip on the booklet. "That so-called Good Book up on the shelf is just a bunch of stories. This right here, this is truth. Bad men, evil men, who'll do

anything they want. They'll steal and they'll kill and they've got to be stopped, whatever it takes. You want to pray? Pray for the guts to stand up to those owlhoots, when the time comes for you to go after them." He shook his head. "I still ain't sure you got what it takes, boy. Maybe you better forget about bein' a Ranger. Maybe you better be a preacher instead. Stick to psalm-singin' and hallelujah-shoutin' with the women while other men do the real work of bringin' law and order to Texas. Maybe that's what you're cut out for." Contempt dripped from his voice as he added, "That'd make your ma right proud of you."

* * *

In the shadowy hallway in the back of the road ranch, Braddock gave a little shake of his head. Most of the time he did his best not to think about his father at all, but the old bastard crawled out of his memories now and then, no matter how hard Braddock tried to banish him.

The old man had always damned Braddock's ma for being weak, but a couple of times after she died, Braddock had seen his father staring at an old picture of his mother, and he'd been crying. He would have denied it, of course, but his eyes had been wet with tears.

Braddock forced his thoughts back into the present. He recognized one of the voices in the front room. It belonged to Jeff Hawley. So Hawley was still alive, against all odds. That was good, because if anybody would know where to find Tull Coleman, it was the crippled outlaw.

The girl didn't struggle as he moved closer to the door and took her with him. It was a little lighter here, and he could see her better. She looked mostly Mexican, but her high cheekbones made him think she had some Indian blood, too. She was young and fairly attractive, but whoring at an owlhoot road ranch like this, those looks wouldn't last very long.

Luckily that wasn't his problem. Finding Tull Coleman and bringing him to justice was.

Even with Braddock's arm across her throat, the girl let out a little squeal of fright when shots roared in the other room. Braddock tightened his grip on her. He heard a heavy thud that was probably a body falling to the floor. Not Hawley, he hoped. He needed Hawley alive for now. He forced the girl forward, pushing through the beaded curtain while the air in the other room was still full of echoes from the gunshots.

Hawley was sitting in a wheelchair behind a table a few feet away on Braddock's right. Braddock's eyes took in the rest of the scene in a split-second's glance.

He saw the corpse lying on the floor in an ungainly sprawl and recognized the man as one of the hombres who'd been playing poker in the Splendid Saloon back in Ozona. That fit right in with his theory about one of the local citizens working with Coleman's gang.

He saw Hawley trying to reload the Smith & Wesson .38 he'd just emptied. Braddock moved on out into the room and said, "Bad idea, Jeff."

Hawley gaped at him in astonishment. "You're not...you can't be..."

Braddock pulled the girl aside so Hawley could see the badge. "That's right. A Texas Ranger."

"But they kicked you out of the Rangers!"

Braddock smiled slowly. Let Hawley make of that whatever he would.

"All the Rangers are gone except for a few..."

Hawley's voice faded as he looked down at the broken-open revolver in his right hand. He held a fresh cartridge in his left hand. Braddock could tell what Hawley was thinking just as clearly as if it had been written down in a book.

The Book of Knaves.

"You're wondering how quick you could put that bullet in the cylinder, close it, and take a shot at me, aren't you, Jeff? You'd have to be mighty fast for it to do any good. How steady are your hands? Is that tequila in your glass? You really think you could even get a shot off before I blow a few holes through you."

"You crippled me. You shot me in the back, you damn coward."

"You'd just tried to kill me, and I didn't want you to get away."

"I swore I'd kill you," Hawley said as he looked down at the gun. "Even if it costs me my life." He raised his eyes and stared at Braddock. "You think I really care if I live or die anymore?"

Braddock saw the resolve in the outlaw's eyes and knew he was going to have to shoot Hawley. He figured he would put a bullet through the man's shoulder—both shoulders if he had to—so that Hawley could still talk.

That was when a big, sloppy figure burst through the beaded curtain behind him, shouted something in a language Braddock didn't understand, pointed a shotgun at him, and pulled the trigger.

Chapter 9

Braddock's swift reaction was the only thing that saved both him and the girl. The fat man obviously didn't care if the shotgun blast shredded her, too.

But Braddock dived to the floor before the load of buckshot had time to spread out much. The girl was underneath him with his body shielding hers. The blast went over both of them and blew a jagged hole in one of the whiskey barrels supporting the bar planks. Rotgut spewed out.

The fat man had fired only one barrel, which meant he was still dangerous. He wore a nightshirt, the bottom of which flapped around pale calves as big around as the trunks of small trees. The man's head was shaped like a barrel cactus and was bald except for some wildly askew strands of white hair. He kept yelling in that foreign language as he started to lower the shotgun's twin barrels toward Braddock.

Braddock angled his Colt up and fired first. The bullet ripped through the fat man's double chin and plowed on up into his brain. He flopped backward as he triggered the shotgun's second barrel. The charge went harmlessly into the ceiling.

Braddock caught movement from the corner of his eye and turned his head to see Hawley turning over the table and shoving it at him. The chess board and pieces went flying. The table hit Braddock and didn't do any real damage, but it did jolt the gun out of his hand.

With the chair's wheels squealing, Hawley rolled toward Braddock and then dived out of the chair. He landed on top of Braddock and clawed at his throat. Hawley's fingers closed like talons on Braddock's windpipe.

Braddock tried to throw Hawley off, but the outlaw clung to him like a leech. As they rolled through the lake of spilled whiskey, they tangled with the girl, who started to scream now that Braddock didn't have hold of her anymore. She raked her fingernails across Braddock's face as she tried to help Hawley overpower him.

Anger surged up inside Braddock. He backhanded the girl and knocked her away from him. Then he hammered a punch into the side of Hawley's head. He had to hit the outlaw twice more before Hawley's grip loosened. Braddock put his hands against Hawley's chest and shoved him away.

Hawley lay there panting. "You...you son of a bitch," he said as Braddock climbed onto his knees and then got to his feet. "You stand there...whole...such a big man." He clenched a fist and pounded it against the floor in frustration as furious tears rolled down his sallow cheeks. "Why don't you come over here and kick me?" he shouted. "Come on! Stomp the helpless cripple!"

"I don't want to stomp you, Hawley," Braddock said. He bent and picked up the gun he had dropped. A glance toward the fat man told him he didn't have to worry about any more threats from that direction. The man lay on his back with a large pool of blood spreading around his head.

The girl was huddled against one of the whiskey barrels, evidently stunned. Braddock didn't trust her, so he kept a watch on her from the corner of his eye as he pointed the Colt at Hawley.

"What I want is for you to tell me where to find Tull Coleman. And don't try to lie and claim you don't know. Neither of us are foolish enough to believe that."

"You really think I'd tell you?" Hawley asked. "I'd die first, and you know that."

"Up to you," Braddock said as he thumbed back the Colt's hammers. Now that the echoes of the earlier shots had died away, the sound was loud in the close confines of the room.

Hawley glared at him for a few seconds, then started to laugh. He propped himself up on one hand and used the other to beckon to Braddock. "Go ahead and shoot," he urged. "Come on, get closer! You don't want to miss, Ranger. Now you be sure to go ahead and kill me this time. Don't foul it up again." He leaned forward. "Come on, you can do it! Just pull that damn trigger, if you've got the guts! Or maybe you're too much of a coward to shoot a man who's lookin' you right in the eye."

Hawley's voice wasn't the only one Braddock seemed to hear at that moment. If he hadn't known better, he would have sworn his father was right there behind him, goading him to shoot the outlaw. Braddock Sr.'s voice was weaker now, slurred as it had been in those last days when the sickness was killing him and whiskey was the only thing that would dull the pain. But even on his last legs he'd been as filled with hate and rage as ever, hatred for outlaws and rage toward the son he thought would never be the man he was.

Braddock listened to both of them, then lowered his gun and slid it back in its holster. He stalked over to Hawley, bent down, and took hold of the outlaw's shirt. He lifted Hawley, who cursed and struck feebly at him. Braddock turned and shoved Hawley into the wheelchair, which rolled backward a little from the impact.

"You're not going anywhere," Braddock said.

Hawley cursed some more, grabbed hold of the chair's arms and tried to shake it in sheer, futile frustration. Then he slumped back and sobbed.

Braddock felt a little sick. There was something repulsive about Hawley. Not his disability so much as it was his reaction to it. The outlaw was like a broken-backed snake, writhing in the dust and biting at things that weren't there.

The girl moaned. Braddock put his hands under her arms and lifted her to her feet. She stood there unsteadily, shaking her head. Finally she lifted it, looked at Braddock, and said, "You hit me."

"I reckon you had it coming. You were trying to help Hawley kill me."

"*You* are the one who has it coming! He was a strong man, and you made him weak."

"He was never strong," Braddock said. "He was a damn outlaw. All he ever did was take advantage of people and hurt them."

Her chin lifted defiantly. "He never hurt me."

"He just hadn't gotten around to it yet." Braddock

changed the subject by asking, "Tull Coleman comes here to see him, doesn't he?"

With a surly glare, she said, "I don't know any Tull Coleman."

Braddock let out an exasperated sigh. "I don't know why everybody feels compelled to lie to help that murdering bastard. What direction does Coleman come from? Just tell me that and I'll go away and leave the two of you alone."

"To do what?" the girl wanted to know. "You killed the Dutchman. This was his place. Now it's nothing."

"Maybe you could run it. You and Hawley."

A shrewd, calculating look replaced the angry expression on her face. "You really think so?"

"Unless that Dutchman, as you call him, has some relatives who can come in and take over everything."

She shook her head slowly and said, "He never said anything about any family."

"Well, there you go," Braddock told her. "What happens here is none of my business. All I care about is finding Coleman."

"If I tell you what I know...you'll drag out that lard-gutted carcass and bury it?"

From the sound of it, she hadn't liked the Dutchman very much. Braddock supposed that he'd treated her pretty roughly.

"Sure," Braddock said. He didn't know if he would keep the promise, but he was willing to make it.

The girl hesitated a moment longer, then said, "All right. It's not much, but I'll tell you."

Before she could say anything else, Braddock heard wheels creaking. He turned to see Hawley rolling toward them. The outlaw had a grimly determined look on his face, but he was unarmed as far as Braddock could see.

Then he realized Hawley held something in his hand. He lifted it, and Braddock saw it was a match. With a flick of his thumbnail, Hawley set the thing alight.

Then he dropped it on the floor in front of him, right into the big pool of whiskey that had leaked out of the buckshot-shattered barrel.

The liquor went up in a huge *whoosh!* of flame that made the girl jump back and scream. Hawley howled with laughter as he rolled forward and the fire engulfed him. His clothes and hair, soaked with whiskey from rolling around in it on the floor, started burning, but he kept laughing.

Braddock grabbed the girl as the flames shot across the floor, following the spilled whiskey, and reached the broken barrel. The liquor that was still in the barrel ignited. It was like a bomb going off, setting the bar on fire and spreading the flames to the other barrels.

Braddock jerked the girl off her feet and dashed toward the door. He slammed through the opening just as more of the barrels exploded behind them.

The force of the blast pushed Braddock forward like a giant hand in his back. He lost his hold on the girl just before he slammed into the ground. As he rolled over he heard what sounded like thunder, but the sky was clear. The rumble came from inside the building, where thick clouds of black smoke were now gushing out of every opening.

The adobe walls wouldn't burn very well, but the roof and everything inside the place would.

Including Jeff Hawley.

Braddock pushed himself up and looked at the inferno. Even if Hawley hadn't been crippled, he never would have made it out of there alive. He was bound to be dead by now...and he had taken his knowledge of Tull Coleman's whereabouts with him.

That realization put a bitter taste in Braddock's mouth. He climbed wearily to his feet and looked around for his hat and the girl. He spotted them both but picked up his hat first, slapping it against his thigh to get some of the dust off of it before he put it back on.

Then he took hold of the girl's bare arm and lifted

her. "Looks like you won't be running this road ranch after all," he muttered. "Time that fire quits burning, there won't be much left."

She spat words at him, but they weren't in Spanish or English like he would have expected. They were German, he realized, the same as what the Dutchman had been shouting at him. She must have picked them up from the fat man while she was working for him.

When her fury finally ran out of steam, she demanded, "What will I do now?"

"Tell me where I can find Tull Coleman," Braddock said.

"Do you *never* think of anything else?"

"Not much," Braddock admitted.

They stood there glaring at each other while the building continued to burn. At last the girl said, "I will tell you what I know, but you must do something for me first."

"What's that?" Braddock asked warily.

"Take me back to the village where I came from. It's just across the border in Mexico, about forty miles south of here."

Braddock frowned. "I don't have time to—"

"There was a man who came to see Señor Jeff every week or ten days. A man lean like you, with reddish hair and a little beard, who was always smiling with his mouth but his eyes were cold like those of a snake."

That was Coleman, Braddock thought. There was no doubt of it in his mind.

"I will tell you which way he came from," the girl went on. "I will tell you everything I heard them talking about...but only after you have taken me back to my home."

"Are you sure you'll be welcome there?" Braddock asked. He knew it was a cruel question and didn't care.

"You mean because I was a whore for the gringos?" She shrugged, and that caused her blouse to slide down on one shoulder. "It doesn't matter. I have nowhere else to go...because of you."

"Hawley's the one who set the place on fire." Braddock grunted. "That Dutchman must have had a hell of a lot of whiskey stored in there."

The girl put her hands on her hips. "Do you want my help or not?"

"How do I know I can trust you?"

"If you take me back to my village, I will have nothing to gain by lying to you."

Braddock supposed that was true enough. What she was suggesting would take only a few days, and he had the time to spare. He had almost nothing but time.

And his duty.

"All right," he said. "We'll go to Mexico. But there's something you have to tell me first."

She frowned warily at him and asked, "What is that?"

"What the hell is your name?"

She looked a little surprised by the question, but she said, "Rosaria. And I know your name. You are Braddock." She paused. "Braddock the bastard."

Without intending to, he found himself smiling.

"As good a name as any, I suppose," he said.

Chapter 10

Rosaria didn't own anything except the clothes she was wearing, and all of Braddock's supplies were in his saddlebags or tied on behind his saddle, so they didn't really need the third horse as a pack animal. Braddock brought it along anyway, leading it with a piece of rope he'd found in the shed. There was tack in there, too, so Rosaria didn't have to ride bareback. She'd straddled the saddle without hesitation, pulling her long skirt up to mid-thigh to free her legs.

They rode side by side in silence starting out, but the quiet seemed to get on Rosaria's nerves. After a while she said, "Hawley told me the man who shot him was no longer a Ranger. He said he and his friend tried to use your own law against you."

"Well, it's pretty clear that didn't work, isn't it?" Braddock said. He was still upset that he hadn't been able to force any information out of Hawley before the outlaw died, so he wasn't in much of a mood for small talk.

Rosaria persisted. "How did you get the Rangers to

take you back?"

"That's my business," Braddock said. He couldn't explain things to this whore. She'd never understand that it didn't really matter what the State of Texas said. He'd never had anything else in his life except being a Ranger, not really, and nothing could change that. The star-in-a-circle badge *belonged* on his chest. If he put it away, if he gave up the only thing that had ever meant anything to him, it would be the same as admitting that his old man was right.

After a few minutes, she said, "Nobody ever tried to stop me from being a whore. All the men in my village seemed to think that was what I should be, from the time I was twelve years old."

Braddock just grunted. He wasn't interested in hearing her life story, any more than he was in sharing his with her.

"My father is a farmer. All the men in my village are farmers. And they are all poor. I have many brothers and sisters, so my father told me since I was the oldest I should do whatever I could to help feed them. I did, but after a while I grew tired of it so I ran away."

"And wound up doing the same thing for the Dutchman," Braddock said, then grimaced because he hadn't meant to encourage her to continue, and he knew she would take his comment that way.

"Sí, only it was even worse. Augustus was a cruel man."

"That was his name?" She wasn't going to shut up, Braddock decided, so he might as well talk to her.

"Augustus Vanderslagen. A terrible name, and a terrible man. Do you know why he tried to shoot you?"

"I figured he was trying to help Hawley."

Rosaria shook her head. "No. It was because you woke him up. He always flew into a rage whenever anything disturbed his sleep, especially if he'd been drinking the night before. Once he chased me all around the place with a meat cleaver because I dropped some empty bottles and woke him. He would have killed me if I hadn't been fast enough to stay out of his reach."

Braddock had to laugh in spite of himself. "I'm glad I shot him, then. I was feeling a little bad about it."

"Were you? Really?"

"Well, no, not much," Braddock admitted. "Once he took a shot at me, I didn't care why. That made him fair game as far as the law's concerned." He paused, then asked, "Why did you stay there, if he treated you so bad?"

Rosaria shrugged, which made her blouse slip

again. "Where else could I go where I would be sure of better treatment? Besides, Augustus wasn't always like that, just most of the time. Every now and then he could be nice. It wasn't like I had a lot of choices."

"Most of us don't," Braddock said. "Fate drives us on, wherever it wants us to go."

* * *

It was mostly flat, open country covered with scrub brush south of Dutchman's Folly all the way to the border, with only occasional ridges and knobs to break the monotony. Late that afternoon Braddock found a place to camp up against the base of one of those ridges. There was no water nearby, but he had a full canteen and most of another one. They would just have to be careful with their water.

Before darkness settled down, he built a small fire to boil some coffee and fry some bacon, then put out the flames. As far as he knew, no one was looking for them, but such caution had become an ingrained habit with him. When you were spending the night out in the open, there was no point in announcing where you were.

As they ate their meager supper, Rosaria sighed and said, "I suppose I will have to sleep on the ground tonight."

"I have an extra blanket you can use," Braddock said.

"Or I could share your blankets," she suggested.

He sipped coffee from the tin cup in his hand, then said, "I don't reckon that'd be a good idea."

"Why? Because I'm a common whore? Because you're too good for me?"

"Because I'm not totally convinced you wouldn't try to get my knife and cut my throat while I'm asleep."

She looked at him expressionlessly for a moment, then laughed. "The big, strong Texas Ranger is afraid of a little Mexican girl."

"I just believe in being careful, that's all."

"You're taking me home. Why would I kill you?"

"I figure you know where you're going," Braddock said. "You don't really need my help to get there. If you rode into that village of yours with three horses and all my gear, I reckon that'd make you one of the richest people there."

She laughed again and said, "You are right about that, señor."

"So just to be sure, I'm going to keep my distance from you. No offense."

"No offense," she agreed with a smile. "You are the one who is missing an opportunity, not me."

"Won't be the first one," Braddock said as he

looked down into his coffee cup.

* * *

"With some hard work, you could really make something out of your father's spread," Laura McElhaney said as she rested her head on George's shoulder. They were sitting on a bench on her pa's front porch, with silvery moonlight washing over the yard in front of them.

"I don't think I'm cut out to be a rancher," George said. "Pa wasn't, either. It was just a place for Ma and me to stay while he was off Rangering."

"That doesn't mean it has to stay that way," Laura said. "I...I could help you. If...if you had a good woman with you...a wife...Oh, George, I know I'm being mighty forward, but I don't want to see you throw your life away."

George stiffened. "Like my pa threw his life away being a Ranger?"

"That's not what I meant—"

"Good Lord, I only put him in the ground three days ago, and you're already telling me to forget everything about him. Forget what he was and what he wanted me to be."

Laura straightened and turned to look intently at him. "That's not what I meant and you know it, George

Washington Braddock. But be honest. He bullied you into deciding to join the Rangers, and everybody around here knows it."

George stood up and stepped over to the porch railing. "I don't want to hear this."

Laura moved beside him and put her hand on his shoulder. "All I'm saying is your father is gone, rest his soul, and you don't have to follow the trail he laid out for you. You can make up your own mind what to do, George."

"I already have." He drew in a deep breath. "I'm riding up to Austin tomorrow to sign my papers with the Rangers."

"You don't have to do that. You can stay here and work the ranch. And if you were to ask me to work it with you, as your wife, I'd say yes."

He'd been courting her, off and on, for two years, and tonight was the boldest he'd ever seen her. She moved against him, slid one arm around his waist and the other around the back of his neck. He felt her body pressed intimately to his and couldn't help but react.

"You know it's what we both want," she whispered.

What she was saying might be true, George thought, but it didn't really matter. His course had been set for him long before. He had grown up seeing the fear and loneliness in his mother's eyes every time his father rode away, and he had sworn to himself that he would never inflict that pain on any woman. His own happiness didn't mean a damned thing when it was stacked up against bringing law and order to the Lone Star State.

He put his hands on Laura's shoulders and moved her away from him. "I'm sorry," he said as he turned toward the porch steps. "I just came by tonight to say goodbye."

"George, you can't just throw away—"

"Goodbye, Laura," he said.

He walked away and didn't look back, even though he heard her sobbing behind him. The easiest thing in the world would have been to turn around and run back to her.

But Rangers didn't do things the easy way.

They did things the right way.

* * *

Braddock gave Rosaria the extra blanket and told her to bed down on the other side of the dead campfire. While she was doing that he checked the horses one last time, then sat down with his back against a rock and the Winchester close beside him on the ground.

"Aren't you going to sleep?" she asked from where

she lay curled up in the blanket.

"Maybe later," Braddock said. "I thought I'd stay awake for a while."

"Why? There are no hostile Indians out here, and the odds of any bandits running across us are small."

"I just like to be careful, that's all."

"A man can be careful all his life and still have trouble come at him when he least expects it."

Braddock thought about what had happened in San Antonio when he brought in Tull Coleman and Jeff Hawley. There was no way he could have anticipated the news about the Rangers being disbanded or predicted the effects that development would have. So Rosaria might be right, he mused, but he still couldn't change what he was.

"Just go to sleep and don't worry about me," he told her.

"I don't worry about you," she said. She yawned sleepily. "I don't give a damn about you, Ranger."

Good, he thought. That was just the way he wanted it.

Chapter 11

San Antonio

Ranger headquarters was mighty quiet these days. The organization had been cut down to four "companies", if you could call them that, of six men each—three officers and three privates. Captain Hughes was still in command of Company D. His clerk had always been one of the Rangers in the company, but now the man was a civilian employee.

The clerk brought in a piece of paper and placed it on Hughes' desk. "Got a letter here for you, Cap'n, from the sheriff of Crockett County over in Ozona."

"He's not complaining because I haven't been able to give him any help tracking down those stagecoach robbers, I hope," Hughes said as he put aside the report he'd been reading and picked up the letter instead.

"Ah...no, sir. He's complainin' because the man you sent roughed up one of his citizens and threatened some more of 'em."

"What?" Hughes frowned. "I didn't send a Ranger

to Ozona."

The clerk gestured toward the letter and said, "Not accordin' to that."

Hughes glared through his spectacles and his frown deepened as he read. His fingers clenched involuntarily on the paper, making it crackle.

"Braddock!" he said. "G.W. Braddock's going around telling people he's still a Texas Ranger?"

"Showin' folks the badge and everything, accordin' to the sheriff in Ozona," the clerk said.

Hughes slapped the letter down on the desk and came to his feet. "We can't allow this," he said. "He's not only pretending to be a Ranger, that says he pistol-whipped an innocent man! Braddock must have lost his mind."

"Sounds plumb loco, all right," the clerk agreed.

"He has to be stopped. He'll have to be brought in so he can't keep doing this." Hughes sighed. "The fool. The blasted young fool. I was afraid this would happen. Doesn't he realize that by adopting this...this masquerade, he's put himself on the wrong side of the law?"

"He's tryin' to hunt down Tull Coleman and his bunch, Cap'n. You said yourself when you heard about that stagecoach robbery and all the killin' that went with it, that it sounded like Coleman's dirty work."

"And I don't doubt for a second that it was, but Braddock has no legal authority to go after them. By doing so, especially the way he's doing it..." Hughes paused and shook his head. "I hate to say it, but G.W. Braddock has made himself an outlaw."

* * *

The man called Wiley was with Coleman as they approached Dutchman's Folly. Everything looked normal from a distance, but as they came closer Coleman noticed that some of the walls had a blackened look to them. A couple of poles had been knocked down in the corral, and the enclosure was empty.

Coleman reined in and said, "Something's wrong."

Wiley brought his horse to a stop as well and asked, "What do you mean, boss?"

"It looks like there's been a fire inside the building. Let me get my spyglass out..."

Coleman took a brass telescope from his saddlebags and pulled it out to its full length. He had taken the instrument from the body of an army officer he had killed several years earlier. The two of them had gotten into a disagreement over a whore at a saloon in Sweetwater. Coleman had had to back down because the son of a bitch had some friends with him, but he'd bided his time and a couple of nights later had caught the man in an alley and put a Bowie knife in his back.

Now Coleman squinted through the glass for a moment and said, "Yeah, the roof's burned and fallen in, looks like. I don't see anything moving around the place."

"What do you think happened to Hawley?"

"I intend to find out." Coleman closed the telescope with a snap and stowed it away, then pulled his Winchester from its saddle boot and nudged his horse into motion again.

Both outlaws had their rifles out and were ready for trouble as they rode up to the building. A couple of black-winged buzzards rose from inside the walls, flying up through where the roof had been, and started flapping lazily away.

"Filthy scavengers," Coleman snarled. He brought the Winchester to his shoulder and fired. Feathers flew and one of the buzzards dropped like a stone. The other bird tried to wheel away, but Coleman worked the rifle's lever, shifted his aim, and downed it, too. The shots were loud in the silence that hung over the deserted and destroyed road ranch.

"I don't much like this, Tull," Wiley said nervously.

"Stay out here, then, if you want to," Coleman said. He swung a leg over his saddle and slid to the ground, landing gracefully with his rifle still ready for instant use. As he strode toward where the door had been, he said without looking around, "I'm going to see if I can figure out what happened here."

Tumbled heaps of ashes were everywhere inside the building. The fire must have been fierce while it was burning, but everything was cold now. Coleman figured the place must have burned days earlier. The smell still hung in the air, but that would take a long time to go away.

Little gray clouds rose around Coleman's legs as he kicked his way through the debris. One of his feet hit something solid, metallic. He pushed some ashes aside, bent and picked up whatever it was he had found, frowning as he tried to figure it out. After a moment he said aloud, "It's a wheel hub."

"What'd you say, boss?" Wiley called from outside.

Coleman ignored him. He kicked around some more and uncovered another wheel hub and some charred remnants of what looked like a chair. Then his foot thudded against something else that rolled.

Coleman recoiled as he realized he was looking down at a human skull that grinned up at him.

"Son of a..." Coleman started to drag in a deep breath, then stopped as he realized he would be breathing ashes and God knew what else. He poked around and found more bones, then straightened and sighed.

He knew he was looking at what remained of his friend Jeff Hawley.

A fire of anger as hot as the conflagration that had consumed Dutchman's Folly began to blaze inside Coleman. He and Hawley had ridden together for several years. Hawley had been the only one left from Coleman's original gang, and even though he couldn't ride with the rest of the boys anymore, Coleman still considered him one of the bunch. Hawley had proven his worth by acting as the go-between for the friends and relatives in the area who fed information to Coleman.

Now he had died, probably in agony as the flames writhed around him, and Coleman wanted to know whether his friend's death was an accident...or if it had been deliberate. Jeff had already suffered so much, being crippled by that damned Ranger's bullet. He hadn't deserved this, too.

Coleman searched through the rest of the devastation and found another charred skeleton lying several yards away from Hawley's. When he turned the skull over, he saw the gaping hole in the back of it. That was where a bullet had exploded out, Coleman decided. Whoever this was—the Dutchman, maybe?—

he'd been shot.

As far as Coleman was concerned, that did away with any possibility of the fire being accidental. Someone had done this. Coleman was determined to find out who and wreak his vengeance on them.

"You all right in there, Tull?" Wiley called.

"No, I'm not all right," Coleman snapped. "Jeff's dead. What's left of him is in here."

"Son of a bitch," Wiley said. His hushed tone made the words sound more like a prayer than a curse. "I found somethin' out here you might oughta take a look at."

Coleman glanced at Hawley's remains. There was nothing else he could do for his friend, not here, anyway. He walked out of the burned building and stomped his feet on the hard ground to get as many ashes off his boots and trouser legs as he could.

"What is it?" he asked Wiley.

"Well, I decided to take a look around out here while you were lookin' in there," Wiley said. He was a tall, burly man with a beard and long, tangled dark hair that fell to his shoulders under a tightly curled Stetson. He pointed and went on, "I found some tracks over yonder."

Coleman's pulse sped up. Tracks might have been left by whoever was responsible for this.

"Show me," he said.

Wiley led him over to the hoofprints. They were several days old, just like the destruction in the road ranch, but it hadn't rained and there hadn't been much wind so the tracks were still fairly clear.

"Three horses, two of 'em carryin' riders and one that wasn't," Wiley said. "I backtracked 'em around to the corral. I'd say somebody tied a mount around there, then took down a couple of poles and got the other horses out. I looked for boot prints but couldn't really make heads or tails of what I found."

"That's all right," Coleman said. "You did good anyway. I'll bet that whoever killed Jeff and set the place on fire took those horses. And then they headed south." He gazed off in that direction, his eyes hooded against the sun glare, as he continued, "Go on back to the hide-out and get the rest of the boys. Then come back here and pick up the trail."

"What're you gonna do, Tull?"

"I'm starting after the bastards now," Coleman said. "I don't know who they are, but I'm going to make them pay for what they did to Jeff."

Chapter 12

"Does this place have a name?" Braddock asked as he and Rosaria rode toward the scattered gathering of adobe jacals. He saw a cantina, a blacksmith shop, and what appeared to be a small store. At the far end of the open area that passed for a street was the largest building in town, a church with a short, blocky bell tower. Next to the church was a well.

Fields with scrawny crops in them surrounded the settlement. Irrigation ditches led from the fields to the Rio Grande, which was a quarter of a mile to the north.

"It is called *La Catedral de la Esperanza*," Rosaria said in reply to Braddock's question. "The Cathedral of Hope, after the church. But everyone usually just calls it Esperanza."

"Looks more like No Hope to me," Braddock said with a wry smile.

"I told you that I was eager to get away from here when I left. What did you expect?"

Braddock didn't answer her question. He said,

105

"Let's just get you back to your family so you can tell me what I need to know and I can be on my way."

The ride from Dutchman's Folly had taken them two full days, plus the remainder of the day they had started out. That meant two nights on the trail. Braddock hadn't slept much either night, just dozed some now and then, because he didn't fully trust Rosaria. She had tried to stab him and then fought on Hawley's side against him. He didn't believe she had miraculously become his friend.

On the other hand, he was the only one around to help her, and he had a hunch Rosaria was pretty damned practical. Like most people in the world, she would use anybody she had to in order to get what she wanted.

At least she had given up trying to coax her way into his blankets at night. She had made some comments in German that he had taken to be pretty derogatory toward his manhood, but things like that didn't bother him. He had more important matters to worry about.

Like finding Tull Cameron and bringing him to justice.

"My father's house is this way," Rosaria said as she led him toward one of the huts on the far side of the village. It wasn't long until nightfall. Men and women were trudging back in from the fields, their shoulders drooping with weariness.

Nearly a dozen small children came running, trailed by several barking dogs, as Braddock and Rosaria rode up to one of the jacals. The youngsters shouted Rosaria's name, leading Braddock to think they must be those younger brothers and sisters she had talked about. She dismounted and began embracing them as they hugged her eagerly in return.

Braddock surprised himself a little by realizing he was glad the homecoming was a happy one for her. Sure, she had tried to kill him, but he supposed that under the circumstances he could understand. She hadn't known who he was when she tried to stick a knife in his back. He was just a tough-looking stranger with a gun, evidently intent on disrupting her life.

And sure enough, things had played out that way.

But maybe she would be better off now in the long run. She hadn't had much of a future waiting for her at Dutchman's Folly.

A tired-looking woman walked up and exclaimed, "Rosaria!" A torrent of rapid Spanish passed between them. Like most folks in Texas, especially the southern half of the state, Braddock had some understanding of Spanish, but the two women were going 'way too fast for him to keep up.

The older woman didn't seem happy to see Rosaria. She waved her hands in the air and practically spat out her words. After a few minutes of agitated conversation, Rosaria sighed and turned back to Braddock.

"My father is dead," she said.

"I'm sorry," Braddock told her. "I lost my pa a few years ago."

"My father was not a particularly good man, but I'm sorry he worked himself to death. And now my mother doesn't want me here. She says I have brought shame to the family."

Braddock wanted her to go ahead and honor her part of the bargain, to tell him whatever she could about the visits Tull Coleman had paid to Hawley at Dutchman's Folly so he could be on his way. However, it was really too late in the day for him to start north again, and since it looked like he'd be spending the night here in Esperanza he supposed it wouldn't hurt anything for him to be sympathetic. He said, "I guess you can stay somewhere else."

"There is nowhere else," Rosaria said with a bleak look on her face. "Maybe I could go to the cantina and do the same things there I did before. The same things I did for the Dutchman. But I had hoped—" She stopped short and laughed bitterly. "You are right,

Braddock. This place should be called No Hope."

His jaw tightened. He felt sorry for her, and he didn't want that. Such an emotion would just interfere with his quest to bring Coleman to justice. He had already spent too much time helping out Rosaria.

"I will go with you," she announced.

"What?" Braddock frowned. "Go with me where? I brought you where you wanted to go."

"But there is nothing here for me. Take me with you, and I will help you find the man you're looking for. The outlaw called Tull Coleman. I can show you the trail he followed when he came to the Dutchman's place."

"You can *tell* me where that trail is," Braddock said. "That was our deal. Nothing was ever said about you coming with me after this."

She shrugged. "Things have changed."

Braddock was so exasperated he felt like turning his horse around and galloping away from here, taking the two extra mounts with him. Since he would have fresh horses he could switch to, he could maintain a fast pace as he rode north again through Texas. He could be back where he'd started in less than two days, he estimated.

But if he did that...he'd be back where he started. No closer to finding Coleman's hideout. Rosaria could at least point him in the right direction.

"I'll think about it," he said grudgingly. "For now...your ma won't even let you spend the night here?"

Rosaria turned back to her mother, and again the rapid Spanish flew back and forth, accompanied by stern shakes of the older woman's head. Braddock didn't need a translation to know what her answer was.

"All right," he said with a disgusted scowl on his face. "Is there a place in town where we can get a room for the night?"

"The cantina. Santo may think I want to come back to work for him, though."

"Well, we'll set him straight about that in a hurry," Braddock snapped.

Rosaria took hold of her horse's reins and swung up into the saddle again. She said, "*Gracias*, G.W."

"It's Braddock. Braddock the bastard, remember?"

"Ah, sí," she said softly. "Such a bastard you are."

* * *

Rosaria's prediction turned out to be correct. The man who owned the cantina welcomed her with open arms and said that his customers would be very happy to see that she had returned. Then he told her to go to his room in the back and wait for him.

That was when Braddock came in after tying the horses to the hitch rack outside, and Santo muttered something about "*Diablo Tejano*" and scurried back behind the bar. Braddock knew the man had seen the badge pinned to his shirt.

He took a silver dollar from his pocket and tossed it to Santo. To Rosario he said, "Tell him that'll pay for our room tonight and also for someone to take care of our horses. And all our gear had better be there in the morning, too."

She smiled and repeated his instructions in Spanish. Santo nodded eagerly. Braddock didn't know if his eagerness came from fear or greed or both and supposed it didn't really matter.

The room was small, with space only for a single narrow bed, a table with a basin of water and a candle on it, and a chair. Braddock thought maybe he could sleep on the floor.

For now he was more interested in the meal of tortillas, beans, chilies, and goat stew that Santo dished up. He'd had a lot of skimpy suppers on the trail in recent weeks, and the food here was good, at least.

It was too bad for Santo, though, that the cantina didn't have any other customers tonight. When Braddock asked Rosaria about that, she said, "It is because word has gotten around that a Texas Ranger is here. My people fear the Rangers because of all the violence in the past."

"The Rangers never hurt any Mexicans except bandits who had it coming," Braddock said.

"That is the way you see it. The friends and families of those so-called bandits may have different opinions."

Braddock grunted. "It's not a matter of opinion. You raid across the border into Texas, you've got to expect the Rangers to come after you."

Rosaria didn't argue with that, and they let the matter drop. Braddock didn't care for the feelings that went through him, though, when he thought about how these people hated and feared him. That just didn't seem right.

When they went back to their room, he lit the candle and then pulled the blanket off the bed and started to spread it on the floor.

"What are you doing?" Rosaria asked.

"I'll sleep down here. You can have the bed."

"Don't be a fool. We will share the bed."

Braddock started to shake his head, but she went on, "You cannot still be afraid of me, G.W. You know I no longer have any place here. The only thing I can do is go with you. Why would I hurt you?"

"You *did* try to put a knife in my back," Braddock pointed out.

"Once! And that was days ago!"

He laughed. He supposed she was right.

She moved closer to him and lifted a hand to rest it on his beard-stubbled jaw. "We are much alike, you and I," she said.

"How do you figure that?"

"Fate has us in its grip, and all we can do is let it carry us along."

"A man makes his own fate," Braddock growled.

"Do you honestly believe that? You said just the opposite before."

Braddock's head was whirling. He didn't know what he believed anymore, and that came as a shock. He had always been so certain that life had one thing and one thing only in store for him: being a Texas Ranger. He had held tight to that, even when everybody seemed determined to rip it away from him. Now he just didn't know anymore...

He put his hand under Rosaria's chin and tipped her head up. "I only believe one thing tonight," he told her. "I believe I'll get in that bed with you."

Chapter 13

Braddock woke and stretched on rough sheets without opening his eyes. As he lay there he thought about the night just past, and as he did he realized with a shock that for the first time in ages, dreams had not haunted his sleep. At least, not any that he remembered. That was a blessing.

He didn't know if that peaceful slumber was because of Rosaria, but he didn't know who else to credit for it. He wondered where she was. He felt around in the bed to be sure that she wasn't there next to him.

Warm light shone against his closed eyelids. The sun was up and spilling through the room's lone window. Maybe Rosaria had gone out to get something for him to eat, or some coffee. Not that he expected her to act like his servant. He didn't want that.

Gradually he became aware that something besides the morning sunlight was coming in through the window. He heard sounds as well: the tramp of many feet, the clinking of harness, the mutter of voices. All

114

that taken together set off alarm bells in Braddock's brain, and his eyes popped open at last.

Braddock had placed his holstered Colt and coiled shell belt on the little table beside the bed so it would be handy. As he bolted upright he reached out and closed his hand around the revolver's grips. Footsteps sounded just outside the door. He jerked the gun from the holster and swung it in that direction.

His finger froze on the trigger as Rosaria flung the door open and hurried into the room. "Braddock!" she exclaimed as she stopped short and stared down the barrel of the gun.

"Damn it!" Braddock had already cocked the Colt. He pointed it at the plaster ceiling and lowered the hammer. "I almost shot you. What's going on out there?"

Rosaria was breathing hard. "Rurales," she said.

Braddock relaxed slightly. The Rurales were Mexico's frontier police force, and this was probably just a routine patrol on its way through the village. He knew they had a reputation for corruption and brutality, but at the same time they were lawmen like he was and he hadn't done anything wrong by being here in Esperanza. True, he had ridden in wearing a Texas Ranger's badge, and as Rosaria had pointed out, the Rangers weren't well liked here, but he hadn't shot anyone or tried to make any arrests.

"Don't worry," he told her. "They won't have any interest in us. We'll just wait until they leave—"

"You fool!" Rosaria broke in. "I was at the well when I saw Santo running to talk to them. He's bound to be telling them that a *Diablo Tejano* is in his cantina. *Presidente* Diaz hates Texans, and Rangers in particular. The Rurale commandant can gain favor with him by arresting you for being across the border without permission!"

Maybe she had a point there, Braddock thought. More than likely it would be better if he didn't fall into the hands of the Rurales. He slid the Colt back in its holster and stood up to reach for his clothes.

"I'll try to get to the horses and make a run for the border," he said. "If I can get on the other side of the river—"

A shout from outside interrupted him. "Ranger!" a harsh voice bellowed. "Ranger, I know you are in there! Come out with your hands in the air!"

Rosaria clenched her hands and looked terrified. "Too late," she said in a half-whisper.

Braddock stepped to the window and glanced out. He was surprised to discover that evidently the cantina was surrounded already. He could see see several men in gray trousers and jackets and matching steeple-crowned sombreros. They wore holstered pistols and carried rifles and looked quite formidable.

If he tried to shoot his way out of here, Braddock thought, he wouldn't make it ten feet before they blew him to pieces.

He had a hollow feeling inside, but he had faced plenty of trouble before and was still here, so he wasn't going to panic. He told Rosaria, "Look, I'll talk to their captain. Maybe I can reason with him. Texas is only a quarter of a mile away, for God's sake!"

"It won't matter," she said as she shook her head. "This is Mexico. And you are a Texas Ranger."

He supposed he should have thought of that before he agreed to bring her here, he told himself. At the very least he should have taken off his badge and pretended to be just a drifter. But it was too late for that now, so he would just have to deal with things as they were.

"You stay in here," he told Rosaria as he pulled his clothes on. "There's no need for you to get involved in this trouble. It's between me and the Rurales."

"I'm the reason you're here."

"Not really," Braddock said. He buckled on his gunbelt. "Tull Coleman's the reason I'm here. All of it comes back to him. Hawley, the Dutchman, all of it." He picked up his hat and put it on, then said again, "Stay here."

"Braddock—" She clutched at his arm as he started past her. He paused and looked down at her, and she put her arms around his neck, pulled his head down, and kissed him with the sort of fierce hunger that a whore wasn't supposed to feel. As she broke the kiss she whispered, "I'm sorry."

"It'll be all right," he said. He wasn't sure he believed it anymore, but he said it anyway.

He walked through the empty cantina. The man in charge of the Rurale patrol was still out front, shouting and demanding that the Ranger surrender. He abruptly fell silent as Braddock stepped through the open doorway.

"Buenos dias," Braddock said with a nod as he confronted the man, who wore the same sort of gray woolen uniform as the other Rurales, only with a few more decorations such as a red sash tied around his waist. He also wore a sheathed sword as well as a revolver. Braddock made a guess as to the man's rank and went on, "What can I do for you, *Capitan*?"

The officer was short and stocky and like most of his men sported a thick, dark mustache. He glared at Braddock and said, "You are a Texas Ranger."

Braddock glanced down at his badge, smiled faintly, and nodded. "That's right. Ranger G.W. Braddock, at your service."

"I am *Capitan* Emiliano Mata, and you are not at my service, señor. You are my prisoner."

Braddock kept a carefully neutral expression on his

face and in his voice as he asked, "Now why would you be arresting me, Captain? I haven't done anything wrong. I haven't broken any Mexican laws."

"You are an American in Mexico without official permission."

"How do you know I don't have your government's permission to be here?"

Mata's face flushed angrily. "I am in charge of this area. I would have been told."

"Well...folks from both sides go back and forth across the border all the time, I suspect, and nobody thinks much about it."

"Not Texas Rangers. Many times in the past the Rangers have come across the Rio Grande and attacked the Mexican people illegally and for no reason."

Braddock had heard about some of those border skirmishes, and he didn't view them the same way Mata did. Right now, however, that didn't matter. Outnumbered the way he was, arguing about the history between their two countries would just antagonize the Rurale captain and make the situation worse.

"I give you my word, Captain, I mean no harm to your people. In fact, I was about to leave Esperanza and head back across the river to Texas. If you'll just let me get my horse, I'll move along and this little incident will all be over."

If by some chance Mata let him go, he could always wait on the other side of the Rio Grande until the Rurale patrol had left the village, then come back across and get Rosaria. By now he had accepted the idea that she would come with him, although he didn't know what he would do with her in the long run.

Captain Mata laughed, but it wasn't a pleasant sound. "This incident, as you call it, will not be over until you have been dealt with by Mexican law. I hereby place you in custody. You will be sent to Mexico City and given a trial." He paused. "Then you will be sent to prison, probably for the rest of your life."

"Because I was a stone's throw on the wrong side of the river?"

"Because you are a damned Texas Ranger," Mata said as his face twisted with hatred.

That hollow feeling inside Braddock had grown until it just about filled him. He knew now there was no way out of this. He was vastly outnumbered, and Mata was determined to impress his superiors by arresting a Texas Ranger.

He didn't suppose it would do any good to tell Mata that he wasn't really—

Braddock's jaw tightened as he cut that thought short. He *was* a Texas Ranger, no matter what anybody else said, and by God, he wasn't going to deny it just to try to save his own hide. The law was more important than that. The law was more important than anything, even his own life.

Especially his own life, because without the law it was nothing.

"Unbuckle your gunbelt, drop it, and step away from it," Mata ordered. He rested his hand on the butt of his own pistol.

"I don't reckon I can do that," Braddock said in a quiet but determined voice.

"Then my men will kill you."

Braddock had moved only a few feet beyond the doorway. He had a hunch that if he acted quickly enough, he could throw himself backward and get behind the protection of the thick adobe walls before the Rurales could shoot him.

But then they would just lay siege to the cantina and pour lead through every door and window, and Rosaria was in there. The fate that awaited him was bad enough, but it would be worse if he was responsible for her death. If he surrendered, the Rurales wouldn't have any reason to hurt her.

"All right, Captain," he said. "Tell your men not to get trigger-happy. I'm going to drop my gun."

"Carefully," Mata advised. "I would rather have a live Texas Ranger to send to Mexico City...but I suppose I could send your head if I have to."

Braddock unbuckled his gunbelt and lowered it to the ground. He stepped away from it and moved toward Mata with his hands held at shoulder height.

"Noooo!"

The scream came from inside the cantina. Braddock jerked around and saw Rosaria charge out into the open. She bent and scooped his Colt from its holster, and as she raised the gun she cried, "Braddock, run!"

"Rosaria, no!" he shouted. He took a step toward her, but it was too late. She had already thumbed back the hammer, and flame spouted from the gun's muzzle.

The next instant, a thunderous roar like the world was ending filled the village as the Rurales opened fire. Horrified, Braddock saw a dozen crimson flowers bloom on Rosaria's white blouse as rifle slugs ripped through her body.

He twisted back toward Mata, determined to kill the captain with his bare hands before he died himself.

That wasn't fated to be, either. Mata had charged at him and was practically on top of him already. The Rurale officer had drawn his sword and swung it in a vicious stroke at Braddock. The blade slammed into Braddock's head and drove him off his feet. Hot blood sheeted down the side of his face as he fell. He saw it splatter redly in the dust around him.

The Rurales closed in. Booted feet crashed into his

ribs. They struck him with rifle butts as well. The brutal torture went on for what seemed like hours before Mata's harsh voice forced the men back.

Standing over Braddock with the bloody sword still in his hand, Mata grinned down at him and said, "Do not think you will be lucky enough to die here, Ranger. You will live to see the inside of a prison cell. But for now, look at the *puta* who tried to help you."

He pointed with the sword, and Braddock seemed powerless not to turn his head and gaze across the dusty ground at Rosaria's body. She lay sprawled on her back with her head twisted toward him so that he could see her face, frozen in lines of agony, and her empty, staring eyes. He wished he could tell her how sorry he was, but it was far too late for that.

Mata was still gloating, but somewhere along in there Braddock passed out, so at least he didn't have to listen anymore.

Chapter 14

Coleman kept his horse moving at a fast pace as he headed for the border. He didn't want to run the animal to death, but the rage he felt at Jeff Hawley's death made him less cautious than he might have been otherwise.

Not foolhardy, though. He didn't try to catch up all in one day. He stopped that night and let his mount rest for a few hours while he grabbed a little sleep himself. But he was up well before dawn, steering by the stars now. The tracks he'd been following headed due south, so he took a chance they continued that way. If he lost the trail, he'd backtrack and find it in the morning. But if his guess was right, he had made up some of the gap between himself and his quarry.

Prey might be a better word, he mused as he rode through the pre-dawn gloom. Because he sure as hell intended to kill whoever was responsible for Hawley's death, slowly and painfully if at all possible.

When the sky grew light enough for him to see, Coleman found the tracks very quickly, confirming that his hunch had been right. The three horses were still heading for the border. He rode on through the day, stopping only when he sensed that his horse was about to give out.

As long as this one got him where he was going, that was all he really cared about. He could put his hands on another saddle mount whenever he got there. After everything he had done in his life, he wouldn't hesitate to steal a horse.

He made camp for a while again that night, then pushed on. At mid-morning, he reached the Rio Grande. He could see the crude adobe structures of a Mexican village not far away on the other side of the river.

Had it been bandits from south of the border who killed Hawley and burned down Dutchman's Folly? That seemed possible to Coleman, although as far as he knew there hadn't been much raiding along the border recently.

There was only one way to find out. The river was low enough here to ford, so Coleman sent his exhausted mount plodding through the water.

He noticed right away that quite a few horses were tied at the hitch racks in front of a building marked simply CANTINA, painted in somewhat shaky letters on the adobe above the arched entrance. Coleman counted eighteen saddled animals. Several men in gray clothes and sombreros lounged around the place, some of them hunkered on their heels in the shade cast by the walls, smoking short brown cigarettes, talking and laughing among themselves.

Coleman saw a few of the villagers moving around, too, going back and forth from the well by the church or visiting the settlement's one store. They avoided the sombreroed men.

Coleman had never encountered Rurales before, but he had a pretty good hunch that was who these men were. Any sort of authority rubbed him the wrong way. The sight of the Rurales made him want to turn around and get the hell back over the border.

The tracks had led across the river and into this village, though. The men he was looking for were here, and Coleman didn't intend to leave without them.

The Rurales paid no attention to him as he rode up to the store and dismounted. He would have preferred going into the cantina—it was always easier to pick up information in a place where men were drinking—but he didn't want to risk it. Maybe he could find out what he needed to know in here.

The inside of the place was cool and shadowy, full of the smells of coffee and peppers and spices. Coleman didn't see any customers, but a squat, bald man with a dirty apron over his clothes stood behind a counter in the back. A look of alarm appeared on his face as Coleman approached him.

Coleman put a friendly grin on his face and tipped his hat back. He could be plenty charming when he wanted to.

"Howdy, amigo," he said. "How are you today?"

"You are a Texan?" the storekeeper asked nervously.

"That's right. Is that a problem? I didn't think folks paid too much attention to the border around here."

"Today is not a good day to be in Esperanza," the man said. "The Rurales have captured a Texas Ranger who had no right to be here. You...you are not one of those devils, are you, señor?"

"Me?" Coleman said. "Do I look like a Texas Ranger?"

"You don't look that much different from the man who was captured by *Capitan* Mata. You are the same sort, I think."

The storekeeper turned his head and glanced toward a barred door behind him. Coleman wasn't sure why he did that, but the gesture seemed to have some meaning.

"Now hold on a minute," Coleman said. "I'm not sure I take kindly to being told I remind somebody of a Texas Ranger. I've had my own run-ins with those boys. What happened to this one?"

The storekeeper licked his lips and nodded toward the door. "He is locked up back there in my storeroom.

El Capitan told me that if anything happened to him, he would have my head. And I believe *Capitan* Mata. He is a very hard man. You don't want him to find you on this side of the border, señor. Please, if you need supplies, tell me what they are. I will gather them, and then you should get back across the border as quickly as you can!"

"Tell me more about that Ranger," Coleman insisted. Something stirred in the back of his mind, something he couldn't quite bring himself to believe, but he wanted to hear more with his own ears.

"He is tall and lean. Like you. His hair is brown, without the red in it like you have. And he has a mustache."

That sounded like...No, it couldn't be, Coleman thought.

The storekeeper went on, "When he was talking to *Capitan* Mata, he said his name was...Braddock, I think."

Coleman stood there like he'd been punched in the gut. He had trouble getting his breath for a moment. His pulse hammered in his head. When the reaction settled down, he said to the storekeeper in a flinty voice, "Tell me what happened here. Tell me all of it."

That didn't take long. When the storekeeper was finished with the tale, Coleman was convinced it really had been none other than G.W. Braddock who had ridden into Esperanza with one of the village girls who had gone off to be a whore in Texas. The girl was dead now, and Braddock, wounded by the Rurale captain, was locked up only a few yards away. Coleman trembled with the desire to stalk over there, open the door, and empty his Colt into Braddock.

There were a couple of reasons why he didn't do that. One was the knowledge that the shots would bring the Rurales on the run, and in all likelihood he would never leave this village alive.

The other was curiosity. Coleman knew good and well that Braddock wasn't a Texas Ranger anymore. Why was this Captain Mata so sure he was? Coleman wanted an answer to that riddle.

He also wanted to get Braddock out of here and back across the border, so he could deal with the bastard in his own time and on his own terms. But again, if he tried to bust Braddock out of captivity, the Rurales would kill him. The odds were just too high.

But Frank Wiley and the rest of the gang were on their way here, Coleman thought with a smile.

And when they arrived, the odds would be totally different.

* * *

A groan welled up from somewhere deep inside Braddock. Part of it was due to the terrible pain that filled his head, but mostly it was composed of despair and sorrow. As soon as he'd returned from the welcome oblivion of unconsciousness, he had remembered how Rosaria died.

He hadn't cried over his ma's death, or his pa's. He hadn't shed tears like that since he'd buried his dog. His father had driven that out of him. So his eyes remained dry now. He wasn't going to cry over a whore, even one he had come to like a little. But she had died trying to help him, so inside he mourned.

A little scurrying noise made him lift his head and open his eyes. He was in a small room somewhere with adobe walls, a hard-packed dirt floor, and a thatched roof with enough gaps in it to let in several shafts of sunlight. Burlap sacks of grain were stacked against one of the walls. A rat perched atop one of the sacks it had evidently just torn open. Its beady eyes stared at Braddock for a second, then it darted away, disappearing through the rip in the sack.

"Eat yourself to death, you furry little bastard," Braddock rasped. His voice sounded foreign to his ears.

He sat up, which made the storage room that was his makeshift prison spin crazily around him for a moment. He lifted a hand to his head where it throbbed the worst and his fingers touched cloth. A quick exploration told him that a rag of some sort had been tied around his head to serve as a bandage over the gash Captain Mata's sword had opened up. The cloth was crusty with dried blood. Braddock knew he had been unconscious for quite a while.

When his head settled down he looked around and tried to figure out if there was any way out of here. He assumed the heavy wooden door was barred on the other side, and there might even be a Rurale standing guard out there, too. The storeroom didn't have any windows. He might be able to tear a big enough hole in the roof to climb out...if he could stack up those grain sacks high enough to reach it.

But even if he succeeded in doing that, Mata's whole patrol was probably still in the village. He'd have to get through them and then make a dash for the river, more than likely on foot.

The odds of him getting away were so slim as to be non-existent.

But at least if he tried to escape, he could force them to kill him quickly, rather than having to endure a years-long death in captivity in some hellhole of a Mexico City prison. That was what he was going to do, Braddock decided. He would go out fast, and if he could get his hands on a gun before he died, he would take some of the brutal sons of bitches with him.

He tried to stand up. That was a bigger job than it sounded like. Every muscle in his body was stiff and sore from the beating the Rurales had given him. He had to rest both hands on the rough wall and lean against it to steady himself as he climbed slowly, inch by inch, to his feet. By the time he was upright he was covered with sweat and his chest heaved from the exertion.

Braddock sleeved some of the moisture off his face and waited until his heart stopped racing before he tried to move again. The room wasn't spinning around any more, either. Carefully, he moved over to the sacks of grain and started rearranging them to form a slope he could climb to the roof.

He disturbed the rat, who burst out of one of the sacks and scurried into a corner. Braddock smiled grimly and said, "I know how you feel."

Then he heard voices on the other side of the door. His heart sank as the bar scraped in its brackets. That meant it was being taken down, and the door was about to be opened. Braddock set himself and got ready to charge out as soon as he got a chance. He would go ahead and make them kill him right here and now.

The door swung back. Braddock lunged forward through the opening, and as he did he spotted Captain Mata standing there with pistol in hand, pointing the weapon at him. Braddock's face twisted in a snarl as he braced himself for a bullet's impact.

Instead something slammed into his back and knocked him down. Fresh bursts of pain exploded inside his head as he crashed to the floor. His muscles refused to work. Hate and rage could accomplish only so much.

Strong hands closed around his arms as two of the Rurales grabbed him and jerked him to his feet. Mata smirked at him and waved a finger back and forth.

"You don't get off that easy, Señor Ranger," he said. "Take him out and put him in the wagon."

This was the first Braddock had heard about a wagon. He wasn't surprised, though. They would have had a harder time keeping him from escaping if he'd been on horseback. That was why he had commandeered a wagon to transport Tull Coleman and Jeff Hawley when he'd captured them. And of course Hawley had been in no shape to ride, what with Braddock's bullet in his back...

The men holding Braddock marched him out through the store and into the street. The Rurale troop was gathered there, most of them already mounted. A couple of men were seated on the driver's box of a wagon with its tailgate down. Another man waited in the back of that wagon with a length of chain in his hands. The chain had a shackle at each end.

Braddock saw the steel ring mounted in the middle of the wagon bed and knew they were going to chain him to it. This was his last chance, he thought desperately. Once he was shackled like that, he'd never get a chance to fight back. They would be able to take him wherever they wanted and do anything they pleased to him.

His captors lifted him, flung him into the wagon. He lay there with his brains screaming commands at his muscles. *Fight! Fight, damn you!*

The Rurale with the chain grinned down at him and said something in Spanish. Braddock was too stunned to follow the words very well, but he understood just enough to know that the man was taunting him, daring him to fight, making fun of him for being a Texan...

Braddock was trying to summon the strength to get up off the wagon bed and throw a punch, just one punch, when a shot blasted and the head of the Rurale looming over him exploded like an overripe pumpkin.

Chapter 15

The Rurales weren't expecting any trouble. That was obvious from the way they stood around gaping for several seconds while more shots rang out and half a dozen of them fell to the onslaught of lead.

The man who'd been about to shackle Braddock to the wagon dropped the chain as he died. Braddock grabbed the chain out of mid-air, and it was as if the links served as a conduit for strength to pour into him from somewhere. He surged up in the wagon bed and lunged at the two men on the seat as they tried to turn around toward him. One of them clawed at the revolver on his hip.

Braddock slashed the heavy chain across the man's head. The sombrero absorbed some of the blow's force, but it was still enough to knock the man sprawling onto the horses hitched the wagon. Spooked, the animals let out shrill whinnies and charged forward.

Braddock almost went over backward as the wagon lurched into motion, but he caught his balance and backhanded the other Rurale with the chain. This time he caught the man on the jaw, which crunched and shattered under the impact. The Rurale slumped to the floorboard, groaning thickly as blood welled from his mouth.

The wagon swayed back and forth as it raced along the street toward the church. Braddock held the chain in his right hand and used the left to grab the back of the seat and brace himself. As he passed the jacals, he caught glimpses of men using the huts for cover as they continued their attack on the Rurales. Rifles spat fire and lead, and more of the Mexican lawmen fell.

For a second Braddock thought that the peasants who lived here had risen against the brutal authorities, but he saw that wasn't the case. His rescuers were gringos like himself, and his heart leaped as he wondered if the Texas Rangers had discovered somehow that he was a prisoner and had come to rescue him.

Then he spotted Captain Emiliano Mata and forgot all about such speculation for the moment. The officer was running toward the church, the same direction the runaway wagon was going. Maybe he intended to seek shelter there. Braddock didn't care. The wagon was about to overtake Mata, and as it did Braddock put a booted foot on the sideboards, levered himself up, and launched himself in a diving tackle.

He crashed into Mata from behind and drove him to the ground. The shock sent jolts of pain through Braddock's head, and he felt fresh blood running down his face from the sword wound. He ignored that and scrambled after the chain he had dropped as Mata rolled over and tried to get his pistol out. The gun cleared leather just as Braddock grabbed the chain and swung it.

The chain slashed across the wrist of Mata's gun hand. He screamed as the revolver flew from his fingers. Braddock swung the chain back, aiming at Mata's face, but the captain got his left arm up in time and the chain wrapped around it instead. He used that to jerk Braddock toward him and met the Texan with a vicious kick to the belly. Braddock gasped and doubled over, but he didn't lose his grip on the chain. He shook it loose and struggled to his feet.

Mata came up, too, dragging his sword from its scabbard. He hacked frantically at Braddock, who flung the chain up and blocked the blade with it. For a long moment the desperate battle surged back and forth, Mata slashing and thrusting with the sword while Braddock used the chain to parry it.

Then the blade went *through* one of the links of the chain, and Braddock was able to twist it out of Mata's hand. He tossed both chain and sword aside as Mata came at him, punching and kicking. It was a near-miracle that Braddock had been able to put up as much of a fight as he had, injured as he was, and now the fuel of hatred and desperation was running out. He had to give ground before Mata's ferocious attack. He tripped on something, lost his balance, and fell backward.

What he had tripped on was Mata's sword, and as the Rurale captain rushed in to try to capitalize on what he saw as a momentary advantage, Braddock scooped up the sword and thrust up and out with it. Mata couldn't stop in time. The blade went into his belly and sliced through his guts before scraping off his spine and then ripping out from his back. He shrieked and pawed at the sword, but he couldn't pull it free. All he succeeded in doing was slicing open his fingers on its keen edge.

Braddock gave Mata a shove to the side. The captain collapsed, curling around the agony in his belly and dying in that position. His death wouldn't bring Rosaria back, so Braddock took no real satisfaction in it, but Mata had gotten what he deserved, anyway.

And this slaughter of Rurales would cause an unpleasant incident between the governments of the

United States and Mexico, especially if Braddock's rescuers really were Texas Rangers. Politics was the least of Braddock's worries just now, however. He felt like he might pass out at any moment.

The shooting in Esperanza had just about died away. He turned slowly to gaze along the street. The men who had saved him from spending the rest of his life in a Mexican prison had emerged from cover now and were stalking among the bodies of the fallen Rurales, casually finishing off any of the Mexicans who were still alive. Braddock didn't recognize any of them, but blood was dripping into his eyes, causing a red haze that made it difficult to see clearly. He tried to wipe some of the blood away as he stumbled toward the men.

"Thank you," he croaked as he approached several of them. "You...you saved my life."

The men turned toward him, and Braddock stopped like he had run into a wall.

Tull Coleman grinned at him and said, "Why, you're mighty welcome, Ranger Braddock. Couldn't have no dirty Mexicans killing you when I want to do it myself."

* * *

Braddock was in hell. At least, it would do until the

real thing came along.

His arms were stretched out to the sides and tied to the posts that held up the roof over the well. He had hung there all day as he watched Coleman and the other outlaws brutalize the villagers and loot the place of its meager valuables. Men who had tried to fight back against them had been gunned down ruthlessly. Braddock didn't want to think about what had happened—and was still happening—to the women and girls of the village.

And all of it because of some politicians and lawyers who had seen to it that a mad dog like Tull Coleman was turned loose on the world once again. Braddock wished they could see the results of their crusade to bring down the Rangers.

But there was more blame to go around. After having him strung up like this, Coleman had gloated about tracking him here from Dutchman's Folly and sneaking into the village with the rest of the gang. If Braddock hadn't been so determined to bring Coleman to justice, he wouldn't have found Jeff Hawley. If he hadn't gone to the road ranch, he woudn't have met Rosaria. He never would have brought her here, and Coleman and the rest of those crazed killers couldn't have followed them.

So in a way, Braddock's feverish brain concluded,

he was partially responsible for opening the gates of hell on Esperanza.

Now night was falling, and the flames leaping up from several of the buildings that were on fire cast a red glow over the entire village. In that glare, Tull Coleman swaggered toward Braddock, rifle in one hand and bottle of tequila in the other.

Coleman was a little drunk, Braddock saw as the outlaw came to a stop in front of him and swayed slightly. With a big grin on his face, Coleman waved the bottle toward the rest of the town and said, "What do you think, Ranger? How do you like what we've done here? I had to let my boys blow off a little steam after they came all this way to give me a hand. The place'll never forget our visit, that's for damned sure!"

Braddock didn't say anything. He didn't want to give Coleman the satisfaction.

Coleman lifted his Winchester and used the muzzle to prod the badge still pinned to Braddock's shirt. "I don't understand. I know damned well they booted you out of the Rangers. You got no right to wear that badge."

"I'll always have the right to wear that badge," Braddock growled.

Coleman shook his head. "Not according to the law. And you know what that means?" He cackled and poked Braddock with the rifle barrel again. "It means you're an outlaw just like me, Braddock! You're on the wrong side of the law now, too!"

Braddock knew he couldn't go on if he allowed himself to believe that. He couldn't accept it. He knew he had done the right thing by continuing to try to enforce the law, no matter what the damned lawyers and politicians said.

Of course it didn't really matter now, he thought. He was already half-dead, and Coleman would take care of the other half sooner or later...when he got tired of terrorizing the village and tormenting his prisoner.

"What happened to your head, anyway?" Coleman asked abruptly. "You look like some sort of damned pirate from a storybook with that bloody rag around your head."

"That Rurale captain hit me with his sword when they captured me."

"The one you gutted like a fish with his own sword? I liked that, Braddock. It was almost enough to make me like you. I got no use for these damned greasers."

"Raul Gomez rode with you," Braddock pointed out.

"That was different. He was one of us...until you killed him." Coleman grew more serious. "Yeah, you killed Gomez and the rest of my men, even Jeff. It just took you longer to catch up to him."

Braddock shook his head and said, "I didn't kill Hawley."

Coleman snorted. "You don't expect me to believe that, do you?"

"It's the truth. All I wanted from him was information about where I could find you."

"Jeff never would've betrayed me!"

"He didn't," Braddock admitted. "He set himself on fire. I reckon he was tired of living in that chair."

"Where you put him." Coleman's face twisted in a snarl, and for a second Braddock thought the outlaw was going to lift the Winchester and blow his brains out. After everything he had witnessed today, all the death and tragedy and horror, Braddock would have almost welcomed that.

"You're a damned coward."

Braddock shook his head. The voice seemed to come from everywhere and nowhere.

"Nobody has to kill you. You're already dead inside."

"No!" The word tore Braddock's throat painfully as it came out.

Coleman took it the wrong way. He sneered again and said, "Don't worry, Braddock. I'm not going to kill you yet. It's gonna take you a long time to die..."

"You've given up. That's something a real Ranger would never do."

Braddock jerked against the bonds holding him to the well as he tried to get away from the words lashing at him. "Get the hell away from me, old man!" he screamed.

"Old man, is it?" Coleman said. "I'm not that much older than you. And you never did tell me how come you're still wearing that badge."

"How about it, boy? Why do you deserve to wear the badge?"

Braddock's head had sagged forward in exhaustion. Now he found the strength to lift it and gaze into Coleman's eyes as he said, "I wear it because I'm a Ranger. I'll always be a Ranger, no matter what anybody else says. Anybody!"

"You know what you are, Braddock?" Coleman laughed. "You're loco! Plumb out of your mind. That's what you are. I reckon when I do finally kill you, I'll be doing you a favor."

Braddock spit at the outlaw's feet.

Coleman stepped closer, swung the rifle up, smashed the stock across Braddock's face. Braddock hung there, blood dripping from his mouth now as it continued to ooze from his head injury as well. Coleman put his face close to Braddock's, and his lips drew back from his teeth as he said, "Come sun-up, everybody who's still alive in this rathole is gonna die, Braddock. You're going to watch it, and you'll know that it's on your head, you crazy fool. You think about that tonight."

He turned and stalked away, and behind him, barely conscious, Braddock muttered, "I'm a Ranger...a Ranger..."

It seemed like he heard someone say, *"Maybe you are, at that,"* but he couldn't be sure.

Chapter 16

Braddock was in and out of consciousness as the long, hellish night dragged on. He was sure that he hallucinated some due to loss of blood, the punishment he had endured, and sheer exhaustion. That was why he had thought he heard his father talking to him, he told himself. Those words had been figments of his fevered imagination.

Because of that, when he felt something tugging at the bonds around his right wrist, he thought that wasn't real, either.

Finally, when the feeling persisted, he raised his head wearily and turned it to look in that direction. He was shocked to see a shadowy figure crouched behind the well, reaching up to saw at the rope around his wrist with a knife.

Most of the fires had died down by now, so the red glare didn't spread across the entire village anymore. Shadows cloaked this end of the street. Coleman had posted one of the outlaws to keep an eye on him, but the man was leaning against a hitch rack, half asleep after hours of debauchery earlier. He didn't seem to notice whoever it was cutting Braddock loose.

The rope fell away, but Braddock kept his arm raised in the same position. That wasn't easy—after so many hours like this his muscles wanted to just go limp—but he knew that too much movement *would* attract the guard's attention.

Just as the fires had died down, so had the shooting and shouting and screaming. A harsh laugh sounded here and there, but for the most part the village was quiet now. Quiet enough for Braddock to hear the soft whisper of bare feet against the dirt as the shadowy figure moved around the well to the other side. A moment later he felt his rescuer start to cut the rope on his left wrist.

Braddock was at a loss as to who would risk their life to help him. He had no friends in Esperanza. In fact, the villagers who were still alive had good reason to hate him for his part in what had happened here.

But whoever it was, he was grateful to them. He was going to have one more chance—his *last* chance, certainly—to go out fighting instead of submitting meekly to his fate.

The rope around his left wrist came loose. He was free. Outnumbered, unarmed, and half dead...but free.

"*Señor.*"

The whispered voice belonged to a woman, but other than that Braddock didn't recognize anything about it.

"A gun there is...behind the well. Four bullets only...all I could find."

"*Gracias*," Braddock whispered in return, then indulged his curiosity. "Who...are you?"

"Rosaria...*mi hija*."

My daughter...It was Rosaria's mother who had freed him. The woman who had turned Rosaria away...but also the one person in Esperanza who probably had the most reason to hate him, for the part he had played in Rosaria's death.

"These hombres...*malo. Muy malo*."

Nobody could argue with that. Tull Coleman and his gang were very bad, all right. The baddest of the bad, Braddock thought.

"You kill them?" the woman said.

"As many as I can," he promised.

"*Bueno*. And you will die, too, I think."

Braddock understood now. She hated all of them, all the gringos who had brought their private feud to this village and caused its ruin. She was unleashing Braddock on them so he could kill as many of the outlaws as possible before he died himself. From her standpoint, that was about all the revenge she could hope for.

He would do his best to deliver it for her. For the woman's sake...and for Rosaria's.

"Distract the guard for a second," he told her, not knowing if she understood that much English. "Give me a chance to get my hands on that gun."

She made no reply, but he heard her feet shuffling as she retreated from the well. He waited, and a moment later she came into view at the corner of his eye, walking toward the guard.

The man straightened from his casual pose when he saw her coming. She stopped when she was between him and Braddock and started haranguing him, waving her arms in the air as she ranted at him in Spanish.

"What the hell," the guard said. "I don't understand what you're goin' on about, you Mex bitch. Why don't you just skedaddle?"

Rosaria's mother kept it up, and while she was doing that Braddock lowered his arms and slipped around to the back of the well. He was unsteady and had to brace himself with one hand on the low stone wall around the well while he felt on the ground in the darkness for the gun the woman had said was there.

His fingers brushed the barrel and closed around it. He picked up the gun and transferred his grip to the butt. It was an old single-action Colt, but as long as it worked, that was all that mattered. Quickly, he checked the barrel to make sure sand hadn't fouled it and found it clean.

The revolver held four rounds, she had said. Well, he would just have to make them count.

He stepped out from behind the well. The guard finally noticed him, eyes growing big as he stared over the woman's shoulder. He must have figured out what she'd been doing, because he jerked up the rifle he held and used it to batter her aside, shouting, "You damned bitch!"

Braddock had to use both hands to aim and fire the Colt, but he squeezed off a shot before the guard could do anything else. Because of the uncertain light he aimed for the biggest target, the man's torso. As the gun in Braddock's hand blasted, the guard staggered. Braddock knew he'd hit the man. But the guard wasn't down, and he managed to fire the Winchester. The slug chewed splinters from one of the well posts next to Braddock.

Braddock had already thumbed back the hammer. He fired a second shot, and this one knocked the guard over on his back. Braddock stumbled forward as he eared back the hammer again. The guard lay there gasping and arching his back like a fish that had been hauled out of a pond. He gave a gurgling groan and then sagged limply on the ground.

Braddock stuck the old revolver in the waistband of his trousers and bent to pick up the guard's fallen rifle and jerk the man's pistol from its holster. While he was doing that, the woman climbed back to her feet.

"Kill them all," she said.

"That's the general idea," Braddock said.

But it wouldn't be easy, the shape he was in, outnumbered as he was. The two shots hadn't drawn any attention so far. Shots had been ringing out all over the village all night as the outlaws wreaked their havoc. That respite wouldn't last, though. In a minute or so somebody would realize they had heard both a rifle and a pistol, and they would come to see what the exchange of shots had been about. Not everybody would be so sated by booze and violence that they couldn't think straight.

"You'd better get out of sight," Braddock went on. "*Gracias*."

If he'd had any doubts about the way she felt toward him, the way she spat at his feet before she scurried off erased them. To her he was just the lesser of two evils, a blunt instrument to be used against the men she despised even more.

That was all right with him. Carrying the weapons he had taken from the guard, he trotted off into the shadows.

Judging by the stars, it was a couple of hours until dawn, and he had a lot of work to do in that time.

* * *

The cantina had a back door, Braddock recalled, so he circled toward it. Some of the outlaws were bound to be there, and Coleman might be one of them.

While he wanted to kill as many of the gang as possible before they got him, his main goal was to put a bullet through Tull Coleman's brain. He didn't need some sort of dramatic showdown. If he had the chance to shoot Coleman in the head from behind, he would take it. All that mattered was putting him down like a hydrophobia skunk, so he couldn't spread any more of his evil through the world.

He eased the building's rear door open and slipped into the darkened hallway. Enough light came through the beaded curtain at the other end for him to see the door of the room where he had spent the night with Rosaria, and that caused his guts to twist for a second. It was hard to believe that less than twenty-four hours ago she had still been alive, snuggled warm and vital against him in the narrow bunk.

The room was occupied now. Braddock heard sobbing from inside, along with a man's harsh, panting breath. Moving soundlessly, he stepped through the door and let his eyes adjust to the darkness. He could make out the entwined shapes on the bed. He knew from the crying that it wasn't the girl's idea to be here.

Braddock moved closer to the bed and raised the rifle in both hands. He would have to strike swiftly and surely to avoid raising a commotion. When he was as sure of his target as he could be under these circumstances, he brought the Winchester's butt crashing down on the outlaw's head.

Bone shattered under the blow, and the woman screamed as the man collapsed on top of her. The scream wouldn't draw any attention from the other outlaws in the place, Braddock thought. At least he hoped it wouldn't.

He had put so much effort into the blow that he almost fell. He caught himself with one hand on the bed and then reached past the dead man to clamp that hand over the woman's mouth so she couldn't raise any more ruckus. He leaned close and whispered, "I'm a friend. Amigo. I won't hurt you. You understand?"

She nodded hesitantly, so Braddock risked lifting his hand. Other than breathing heavily, she didn't make a sound.

He grasped the dead man's shoulder and rolled him off the bed. The corpse thudded to the floor. The sound made Braddock wince, but it couldn't be helped.

"You speak English? How many more of them are here?"

She understood enough to grasp the meaning of his question, although she answered in Spanish. "*Tres.*"

Her voice was young. How young, Braddock didn't want to think about. Instead he whispered, "*Gracias.*"

The man's trousers were down around his ankles. It was a repulsive task, but Braddock felt around until he located the man's holstered gun and also a sheathed knife. He unbuckled the belt and strapped it around his lean hips. He was turning into a walking armory, he thought as a faint smile tugged at his lips in the darkness. Now he had a rifle, three handguns, and a knife.

He would probably need all of them before the night was over.

"You run on home," he told the girl. She hurried out, pulling a ripped dress around her as she headed toward the back door.

Braddock turned toward the front of the cantina.

The other rooms here in the back seemed to be empty, and he saw why when he reached the curtain and peered through the screen of beads. The other three outlaws sat at a table, passing around a bottle of tequila. They had either already taken their turn with the girl, or were waiting for it.

Braddock spotted Santo slumped forward over the bar. At first he thought the proprietor was sleeping, but then he saw the drops falling slowly from the puddle of blood that had reached the front edge of the bar. More than likely the outlaws had cut Santo's throat and he'd collapsed over the bar as he died. He was still balanced there.

None of the men at the table was Tull Coleman. But they were all killers, rapists, arsonists, and thieves, Braddock told himself. As a Texas Ranger, it was his job to bring them to justice. Here and now there was only one way to do that. The thought propped up his fading strength.

He hoped they were drunk enough that their reactions wouldn't be very fast. Right now, his sure weren't. His eyesight wasn't too clear, either. Luckily, the range was only a matter of a few yards.

He stepped through the curtains. The outlaws had to have heard the beads clicking together, but they would think it was just their friend coming back from having his fun with that poor girl.

Braddock lined his sights on the back of the man closest to him and pulled the trigger. The Winchester cracked and blew the bastard's brains out. The outlaw fell forward across the table as blood, bone fragments, and gray matter sprayed in the faces of his companions.

They were shocked enough that Braddock was able to lever the rifle and shoot one of them in the chest before the third man finally reacted and surged up from his chair as he clawed out the gun on his hip. Braddock fired and turned the outlaw halfway around with the shot. He levered and squeezed off a fourth round. This one struck the last man in the jaw and tore it away, leaving him to make a strangled sound that tried to be a scream but couldn't quite make it. As he made a last-ditch attempt to lift his gun, Braddock shot him in the head and dropped him for good.

That flurry of shots, on top of the ones earlier, was bound to bring attention. Braddock lowered the rifle, wheeled around, and hurried out the back of the cantina. He heard men shouting in alarm somewhere along the street.

Any time now, somebody would notice that he was no longer tied to the well. They would figure out that he was the one stalking through the shadows and killing them.

He smiled bleakly as he imagined how well Tull Coleman would take *that* news.

Chapter 17

"Find him!" Coleman screeched as black fury threatened to consume him. "Find him and bring him to me!"

How the hell did Braddock do it? he asked himself as he stalked back and forth in front of the well where the former Texas Ranger was supposed to be tied. Braddock had been stripped of his badge and disgraced, yet he had come back from that to cause more trouble for Coleman. He had survived a run-in with the Rurales, including an ugly head wound from a saber, he'd had the hell beaten out of him several times, and he'd been strung up like a sack of meat.

And yet Braddock was still alive, and a handful of Coleman's men were dead, including the one who'd been guarding the former Texas Ranger.

The bastard had had help to escape. Coleman knew that because one of his men had brought a torch and they had found the pieces of rope that had been used to tie Braddock to the well. Those ropes had been cut. One of the villagers had dared to set him free. That surprised Coleman. He had believed that the survivors were thoroughly cowed.

He felt better than ever about his decision to kill everybody here and finish burning the place to the ground. They had it coming, the dirty greasers, he thought.

Some of his men had already started looking for Braddock, but the others were just standing around looking confused. They'd had too much to drink, sated their appetites too much. They were groggy with their own decadence. Coleman waved an arm at them and yelled, "What the hell are you waiting for? Spread out and find that son of a bitch!"

The men began to disperse cautiously. Most had worried looks on their faces. Five of their pards had been struck down by an avenging force out of the shadows, and it might come for *them* next. There was just no telling.

Shots blasted at the other end of town. "He's here!" one of the outlaws screamed. "He's—"

* * *

Braddock looped his arm around the man's neck, jerked his head back, and ripped the knife across the tight-drawn throat. Blood gushed blackly, fountaining out a good ten feet. Braddock let go of the outlaw and stepped back as the man dropped to the ground to gurgle out his last few breaths.

Two more members of the gang were lying in a tangled sprawl behind him where he had gunned them down. Neither had moved since they fell, so Braddock was confident they were either dead or dying. He left them there and trotted off into the deeper shadows.

He heard more of the outlaws coming, but they weren't charging ahead blindly anymore. They were being careful now because he had managed to spook them, which was exactly what he wanted.

A few minutes earlier, he had spotted Coleman at the other end of the street and seriously considered taking a shot at the boss outlaw. He'd decided against it because he was just too damned shaky. He wasn't sure he could hit the target at that range. When the time came for him to finish off Tull Coleman, he wanted to make sure of the kill.

On the other hand, he had to wonder how much longer he could continue like this. He was operating now on pure hate, and that wouldn't keep him going forever. Sooner or later—probably sooner—his battered body would collapse and there would be nothing he could do to stop it.

Coleman had to be dead before that happened.

Braddock leaned against the rear wall of a burned-out hut and closed his eyes for a moment to gather what strength he had left. As he stood there he heard rough voices approaching. He set the rifle against the wall and drew two of the revolvers.

One of the men coming around the hut said, "I'm thinkin' about saddlin' my horse and gettin' out of here. Seems to me this place must be cursed. How could it not be, with all the dyin' that's gone on since yesterday mornin'?"

"You try to leave now before we catch that damn Ranger and Tull's liable to shoot you himself. I never saw anybody with such a powerful hate for a fella."

"Tull says he ain't really a Ranger."

The other outlaw snorted and said, "He's wearin' that star in a circle and it appears he's pure hell on wheels when it comes to fightin'. That says Ranger to me, no matter what anybody else claims."

Even the shape he was in, that put a smile on Braddock's face for a second.

Then as the men came around the corner of the building, he raised both guns, pointed them at the shadowy figures, and began thumbing off shots as fast as he could.

The slugs tore into the outlaws and made them jitter backward in a bizarre dance for a couple of steps before they collapsed. As they fell, Braddock pouched the iron in his right hand and grabbed the Winchester. He dashed across to another half-destroyed hut and clambered over a wall that had fallen in for the most part. He dropped to a knee, rested the rifle on what was left of the wall, and waited.

Three men ran up to the ones he had just shot. As they cursed in surprise at the discovery, Braddock opened fire again. He emptied the Winchester and dropped two of them, but the third man reached the corner of the hut and took cover there as he returned Braddock's fire. Braddock ducked as bullets smacked into the adobe wall near him.

More men shouted nearby, and he heard running footsteps. They were closing in around him now. If he didn't get out, they would trap him here and he wouldn't get to kill Tull Coleman.

With that thought to spur him on, he waited for a lull in the firing from the other hut and then lurched to his feet, vaulted over the wall, and made a dash away from there. He left the rifle since it was empty and he didn't have any more ammunition for it.

A dark shape appeared in front of him. Colt flame bloomed in the predawn shadows. Braddock felt the wind-rip of a bullet past his ear as he triggered the Colt in his hand. The outlaw grunted and spun away.

He hadn't missed many shots tonight, Braddock

161

thought as he kept running toward the old church. It was almost like some other agency was guiding his aim, another set of eyes and hands hovering behind him, directing his bullets.

But that was crazy.

Damned if he was going to give the old man credit for something like that.

A rifle spit fire at him from the right. He heard the whipcrack of the slug as it passed close by. Someone else opened up on him from the left. He was in a crossfire and knew he stood little chance of making it to the church.

Then more shots sounded and a man cried out in pain. Both rifles bracketing him fell silent. Had the outlaws inadvertently shot each other? Braddock had no idea, but he kept moving. He wasn't running now so much as stumbling, but the church was right in front of him. He grabbed one of the double doors at the entrance, jerked it open, and half-ran, half-fell into the stygian darkness inside.

He bumped into something, felt of it and realized it was a pew. As he slid down onto it, he wondered if the priest was hiding out or had been killed by the outlaws. *El Catedral de la Esperanza*, Rosaria had called this place. The Cathedral of Hope. He'd been making a grim joke when he suggested maybe it should be called No Hope, but that had turned out to be right.

As Braddock sat there trying to catch his breath, he heard more shots somewhere outside, followed by the swift rataplan of hoofbeats. Some of Coleman's men must have had enough and were taking off for the tall and uncut despite their fear of their leader. That would make the odds against Braddock a little better. The shots, he decided, were just wild ones as the spooked outlaws blazed away at shadows.

The guns fell silent, and the hoofbeats faded away. A hush settled over the village. Braddock didn't expect it to last for long, and sure enough it didn't.

"Braddock!" That hoarse screech came from Tull Coleman. "Braddock, where are you? Come on out and face me, you son of a bitch! You goddamn phony Ranger!"

Those words made anger well up inside Braddock. Deep down, in his own heart, he still considered himself a Ranger and always would. To have scum of the earth like Tull Coleman accuse him of being a phony was more than Braddock could stand.

He pushed himself to his feet and started checking his guns. Two of the revolvers were empty, and the other held only two rounds.

He had six more cartridges in the loops on the

gunbelt, he discovered when he checked them. And they wouldn't fit the gun Rosaria's mother had given him. Braddock set it on the pew. He thumbed four cartridges into one of the remaining guns and the other two into the cylinder that was already partially loaded.

Eight rounds. They would have to be enough.

"Braddock!" Coleman screamed. He sounded a little closer now, like he was coming toward the church. "Braddock, where are you?"

For a long moment Braddock stood there with his arms down at his sides, a gun in each hand. A bone-deep weariness stronger than anything he had ever experienced filled him. He had absorbed too much punishment over the past few days. Even more than that, he had seen too much death. His soul was awash in fire and blood. His hands would never be clean.

The only atonement he could make, and it was a slight one, was to see to it that Tull Coleman never hurt anybody else.

"Braddock!"

He strode to the church doors, kicked them open, and stepped out as his hands came up filled with the two guns.

"Right here, Coleman!" he cried.

The outlaw was twenty feet away. Braddock didn't see anything else moving on Esperanza's lone street.

Coleman's gun was already drawn, too, and even though Braddock had a slight head start on him, Coleman was in better shape. His gun came level first and flame spouted from the muzzle.

Braddock felt the hammerblow of a slug against his chest and rocked back a step, but he didn't fall. He brought both revolvers to bear on Coleman's chest and squeezed the triggers. The guns roared and bucked against his palms as he fired two shots from each of them.

Coleman jerked back, jolted by the bullets' impact. His gun hand sagged. His Colt blasted again, but the bullet went into the dirt at his feet. His mouth opened, and he rasped, "You...damn...Ranger," before blood welled out over his chin. He pitched forward and landed on his face.

"You got that right," Braddock said.

His strength was finally gone, drained completely from him, and he felt like he might never get it back. The guns still held two bullets each, but he couldn't hang on to them anymore. They slipped from his fingers and thudded to the ground in front of his feet. He reeled backward and the only thing that stopped him from falling was that his back hit one of the church doors, which had rebounded shut after he kicked them open and stepped through. He leaned against it and waited for the rest of Coleman's men to kill him, but nothing happened. The echoes of the shots rolled away, and Esperanza was silent.

Braddock's legs wouldn't hold him up. He started to slide slowly down the church door until he was sitting in front of it with his legs stretched out in front of him. His head drooped, and as he saw the dark bloodstain on his chest he realized the sky had gone gray with the approach of dawn.

There were worse places to sit and wait for death to claim him than the doorstep of a church, he thought. He'd never been a particularly religious man, and after everything that had happened he figured God wouldn't want anything to do with him, if there was a God, but Braddock took comfort in where he had wound up, anyway.

He started to close his eyes, but then something made him struggle to lift his head again. He looked along the street and saw a tall, imposing figure striding toward him through the gloom. Even though the sun wasn't up yet, the star on the man's chest seemed to glow with the reflection of the onrushing day. Braddock's lips were dry and cracked and his tongue was swollen, but he forced himself to whisper, "Pa?"

The man kept coming, tall, so tall, with high-crowned hat on his head and duster sweeping around his legs, and now there were two more men flanking him, just behind him, and they looked much the same, all with badges on their vests, and Braddock realized they weren't ghosts or angels or even demons come to drag him down to hell.

They were Texas Rangers.

That was the last thing Braddock knew for a long time.

Chapter 18

He came to his senses nine days later in a room at the mission with the brown-robed priest tending to him. Braddock figured the padre was going to give him the last rites, but the mild-faced, balding man smiled and said in barely accented English, "You are well on your way to recovery, *Señor* Braddock."

"I'm not...gonna die?"

"We are all going to die sooner or later, *señor*. But my feeling is that *El Señor Dios* is not yet ready for you to depart this earth."

Braddock had a feeling *El Diablo* would be a lot more interested in his final whereabouts, but it seemed wrong to argue with a priest inside a church so he didn't say anything about that. Instead he asked, "Is this Esperanza?"

"*Sí.*"

"What happened...after Coleman and I shot it out?"

"Three men brought you here and asked that I care for you. *Tejanos.* Rangers. Like you."

Not like him, Braddock started to say, then stopped

himself. Maybe it was because he'd been hurt so bad and had been unconscious or at least out of his head for so long, but he was having a hard time wrapping his brain around what the priest had just told him.

"Rangers...here?" he asked.

The padre nodded. "One of them asked me to tell you that Captain Hughes sent them to find you. To...arrest you. But he said that since you were in Mexico, he and his friends had no jurisdiction, no right to take you in."

That legal nicety wouldn't stop most Rangers, Braddock knew, when they felt like they were in the right. He was certain of that because he had bent a few rules himself along the way. But being on the wrong side of the border...that made a good excuse when you didn't really want to carry out your orders. When you weren't sure you'd be doing the right thing if you did.

"They're the ones who helped me," he said in a half-whisper. "When I was fighting Coleman's gang. There really was somebody giving me a hand."

"*Sí, señor.* They trailed you here from a place called..." The priest sounded doubtful. "Dutchman's Folly?"

Braddock leaned back against the pillow behind him and said, "That's right." He could see now what had happened. Word of what had happened in Ozona had reached Captain Hughes, and he'd dispatched a trio of Rangers to bring him in. As limited as the number of men at the captain's disposal was, Hughes must have really wanted him found. The trail had led from Ozona to Dutchman's Folly and then to Esperanza, and the Rangers had arrived just in time to take a hand in the fight, borders be damned.

But then, instead of taking him in, they had left him and asked this priest to nurse him back to health.

He was curious about that, but he wanted to know something else first. "The village," he said. "How bad...?"

"Very bad," the priest said with a solemn expression wreathing his face. "There are many new graves in the churchyard. But those who are left will go on. These are poor people, *señor*. They are accustomed to life handing them more than their share of bad fortune. Their reward will be in heaven, in the time to come someday."

Braddock hoped that was right, for the sake of the villagers of Esperanza. He said, "I'm surprised they don't hate me. I brought all this on them."

The padre shook his head. "No, *señor*. *Capitan* Mata and his Rurales were evil men. So were *Señor* Coleman and his men. You opposed them. This means you are a good man."

Braddock wished it were that simple. But again, he didn't want to argue with a priest...

"You said I was healing up."

"*Sí.* You needed rest more than anything else. And for the wound on your head to be cleaned and stitched. I'm afraid it will leave quite a scar. Your hair may never grow back there."

Braddock shook his head and said, "I don't care about that." He frowned. "I thought Coleman shot me in the chest."

"The bullet barely penetrated. I was able to dig it out. The wound was not a bad one."

That didn't make any sense, Braddock thought. But that was true about a lot of things in his life recently.

"What am I going to do now?" he mused, sighing as he looked out the window.

The priest hesitated. "The Ranger who asked me to care for you...he gave me a message and requested that I pass it along to you when you were in your right mind again."

Braddock wasn't sure that would ever be the case again, but he looked at the priest with interest.

The man went on, "The Ranger declared that he would not arrest you because you were in Mexico, as I told you before, and also because you killed this bandit Tull Coleman, who was very bad and deserved to die. But he told me to make sure you understand...if you ever set foot across the border in Texas again, the Rangers will be waiting for you. He said you should stay in Mexico, if you know what is good for you."

"I can't do my job in Mexico," Braddock growled. "As soon as I'm on my feet again, I'll need to get back to my work."

"I am just telling you what he said, *señor*," the priest said with a shrug and a smile. He started to turn away. "Now I should bring you some soup. You must get your strength back, and that will help." He paused at a little table beside the door. "Oh, yes. The Ranger said you would want this. Actually, he said he was *afraid* you would want this."

Braddock held out his hand, and the brown-robed man dropped something on his palm. As Braddock stared down at the object, he felt a chill go through him. Now he knew why Coleman's bullet hadn't penetrated deep enough into his chest to kill him.

What he held in his hand was his Texas Ranger badge, with a bullet hole punched neatly in the center of the silver star.

About the Author

James Reasoner has been a professional writer for nearly forty years. In that time, he has authored several hundred novels and short stories in numerous genres. Writing under his own name and various pseudonyms, his novels have garnered praise from Publishers Weekly, Booklist, and the Los Angeles Times, as well as appearing on the New York Times, USA Today, and Publishers Weekly bestseller lists. He lives in a small town in Texas with his wife, award-winning fellow author Livia J. Washburn. His blog can be found at http://jamesreasoner.blogspot.com.

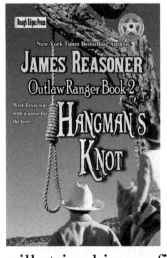

Hell came to Santa Angelina on a beautiful morning, as the Texas settlement was practically wiped out by vicious outlaws led by the bloodthirsty lunatic Henry Pollard. Now Pollard is in jail in Alpine, waiting on his trial and an all but certain date with the hangman. The only real question is whether an outraged lynch mob will string him up first.

Not everyone wants to see Pollard dance at the end of a rope, however. His gang of hired killers would like to set him free, and so would his older brother, a wealthy cattleman who has always protected Pollard from the consequences of his savagery.

Riding into the middle of this three-cornered war is the Outlaw Ranger, G.W. Braddock, who may not have a right anymore to wear the bullet-holed star-in-a-circle badge pinned to his shirt, but whose devotion to the law means he'll risk his life to see that justice is done!

HANGMAN'S KNOT is another fast-action Western novel from New York Times bestselling author James Reasoner. Brand-new and never before published, it continues the violent saga of the Outlaw Ranger.

CPSIA information can be obtained
at www.ICGtesting.com
Printed in the USA
LVHW011040030319
609304LV00013B/544/P